You Think You Know

By

Fina

You Think You Know

By

Fina

ISBN 978-0-6152-0804-6

Manufactured in the United States of America

The situations and characters described in this book are
products of the author's imagination. Any resemblance to
actual events, locales, or persons, living or dead, is entirely
coincidental.

Published by Seven Stages Publishing House, LLC
Cover Photo by Michael's Photography
Edited by Sharon D. Smith

First Edition

Keywords: lesbian erotica, Fina

To submit questions, comments, or concerns about this book
or for information about bulk purchase discounts, please send
an email to inquiries@7stagespublishing.com or write to:
Seven Stages Publishing P.O. Box 1164 Roswell, GA. 30077

What People Are Saying

You Think You Know

By

Fina

INDEX OF EROTICA

I Can't Believe
How Last Night Went

Oh my God, I can't believe how last night went. My sweetheart went to work and in the middle of the night, she came home. I thought I was dreaming when I felt my blanket slowly slide off my body. It wasn't hot enough for the air condition to be on so I had the windows slightly opened to allow the cool breeze to caress me as I slept. I rolled over in the bed to reach for my blanket with my eyes still closed. I felt around both sides of the bed for my blanket, but to no avail. I opened my eyes in frustration and to my surprise, there she was standing over me.

I glanced at the clock on the nightstand. It was 3:00 AM. She climbed on top of me and gently kissed my forehead. Aside from two nights when she was out with the flu, she never missed work. I hoped nothing was wrong.

"Baby, is everything okay? What happened at work? Why are you home so early?"

"Shhhh," she said as she raised her finger and touched her lips.

Her eyes were fixated on mine. It seemed like she could see right through me and know that I was yearning for her. Damn, I wanted her to take me to the land of orgasm. I continued to lay there and submit to whatever she wanted me to do and however she wanted to do it. She started to slowly suck my left nipple and with her other hand, caressed my right breast. Damn, her tongue was so warm. It felt so good to have her soft lips surround my nipples and her warm hands touching my body. I could hardly stand it. She kissed me all over my body and didn't miss a single inch.

She then sucked my fingers, two at a time. I heard her moaning like they tasted good inside her mouth. She soon put my hand on my pussy while she sucked my nipples, which were already dangerously hard. I couldn't believe how wet she made me. Usually penetration would have me this wet, but it felt like a river was flowing between my thighs.

"Play with that pussy, baby," she whispered in my ear.

I must have tasted delicious because she damn near sucked the fingerprints off my fingers. Damn, that shit was turning me on. She moved down to my stomach. Being a plus size girl, I tend to feel a little timid about my stomach. But, she put me at ease and kissed me passionately. She kissed it as if I had a six-pack with the body of a goddess.

I was covered with goose bumps as she worked her way down to the end of the rainbow to find her pot of gold. I say "her" pot of gold because I don't want anyone near it but her. She started kissing and licking my inner thighs. I felt her tongue move closer to my clit and she soon started licking it with the tip of her tongue. Her tongue was so warm on my clit that it responded by standing at attention. She started to eat me as if she was on death row and my pussy was her last meal before dying.

With every lick, I got closer and closer to having an intense orgasm. I could tell she was in heaven, just as I was. She no longer teased me with the tip of her tongue. Instead, I could feel her whole mouth on my clit as she sucked it. Oh my God! I couldn't take it anymore. I wanted to scream.

"Please, please baby," I moaned. "Don't suck. It's making me so weak."

My heart was beating like a drum in my ear. It felt so damn good, I thought I was going to die from the excitement. I grabbed her hands and pulled them up so she could squeeze my breasts. I wanted to rain on her with my love.

I opened my legs wider so she could get all of my juices as they started to come down. Close to the point of no control, I said to her in a faint voice, "yes, yes" just to let her know she was in the perfect spot. I wanted her to squeeze my breasts harder and harder as I reached my orgasm. She knew that I loved that shit and she did exactly what I wanted her to do. I didn't think I could stand but a few more licks. My body betrayed me as my legs began to shake. I moved up on the bed and away from her tornado tongue, but she pulled me back down to her. I couldn't get away. I was her prisoner and she was the warden of my pussy, keeping it under lock and key.

"I can't hold it any longer, baby," I stuttered. My legs shook uncontrollably. My breathing intensified.

"I'm cumming," I yelled out in satisfaction.

She held me for a while until we both fell asleep. Not long after, I suddenly jumped up. My cell phone alarm went off and I looked at the time. Oh shit! It was 9:30 AM and I had to be at work a half hour ago. I couldn't believe she didn't go to work and we spent the whole night making love. Who was I fooling? I hoped she didn't go to work again tonight. But, that wasn't going to happen.

The Lesbian Circle
of Destruction

My name is Fantasy and I've been watching lesbian circles of destruction. I've known for a while that they are connected. I never said anything. Everybody is connected to someone, but it's hard to show it because everybody is lying about something. Here is how it starts.

I've known Smoke for years. I introduced her to Alicia and they have been married for eight years. They were so happy with each other. Everybody wanted a relationship like theirs. Everyone except me.

But who am I? Who am I to tell them they shouldn't have been married. Hell, I knew Alicia had been in a relationship with Smoke's best friend and best man, Dee, for a year before the wedding. Smoke isn't any better because she has been fucking Chantae, Dee's current wife. Chantae just happened to be Smoke and Alicia's wedding planner. Chantae is a patient who often goes to the clinic on 4th Street for a check-up because she's fucking the whole world.

The one person Chantae fucks the most is the nurse, Merri, but Merri is married to a stud named Zoe. Get this shit. Zoe is getting fucked by this stud (yes, that's what I said) named Tee. All I can say is that Tee is fine as hell. Tee's wife, Stephanie is a mail carrier who delivers more than mail to the Williams Law Office on 2nd Avenue.

Ms. Williams is a successful attorney and she has everything a woman could ever want. However, she still isn't happy. No matter how successful she is, she still enjoys fucking goons and likes to get high.

Ms. Williams is fucking Murder who is a big time power dealer on the southside of town. Well, no one loves a goon more than your girl, Fantasy. So, when Murder bumped into me at the club one night, that was all she wrote. I will seek and destroy until I get what I want and I wanted Murder. I watched her for a while. She always rocked Coogi, kept a pair of J's on her feet, and had at least 14 gold teeth. She drove a Chevy Caprice on 28s. Anyone who knows me knows that nothing turns me on more than to see a girl be more of guy than a real guy.

We hooked up and started talking and she told me about this married chic that she's been chilling with. To make a long story short, after the bullshit talk was over, she took me to a nearby hotel room and she fucked the shit out of me.

When she took a shower, my nosey ass looked in her bag. What did I see? A picture of her and Alicia's ass hugged up like they're a couple. I just got sick to my stomach because I've just completed the circle of destruction. I know it's wrong, but yes, I fucked Smoke on their wedding day. So now the circle is complete and I hate it.

Are you in a lesbian circle?

You Never Know
What Will Happen

I walked in on my homegirl having sex. Damn, all this time I thought she was the submissive one in her relationships. From what I could see, this bitch was the one laying it down in the bedroom. Seeing her right then was the moment I knew I had started my vacation on a good note.

I met my homegirl, Samantha, about fifteen years ago. We worked together at a call center in Atlanta for about four years. She was married and her husband was a sergeant stationed in the army on a military base in Ohio. I didn't see her for a long time. However, we managed to keep in touch.

Although she didn't agree with my lifestyle, Sam was still my homegirl. Sam knew I liked women, but she didn't know that she was the one I truly liked a lot. Sam was fine as hell. She was tall, about 5'8", brown skin, and she was about a size 8. She was definitely not a thick woman. Besides, I wasn't into skinny chicks, but that bitch had a beautiful body.

Unfortunately, I couldn't reveal my attraction for her. She wasn't into women at all unless you want to count this one time a long time ago when we planned to go to the mall. We had just taken a shower at her house. I went first and then she went. When she stepped out of the shower, I was putting on some of my favorite lotion by Baby Magic. She came out the shower and we continued to laugh like we normally did while talking about shit and joking about the haters at work. It was just the normal "who's fucking who" type of talking. From out of nowhere, she asked me to put lotion on her back. As I grabbed the bottle, it fell out of my hand. I reached down to pick it up. On my way back up, Sam turned around and her pussy was staring me in the face saying "eat me."

If there was one thing that could make me excited and wet, it's a sexy, clean, low shaven pussy. She was fine as hell and her coming out naked and standing in front of me like that wasn't making it any easier for me to hide my feelings for her. I couldn't help myself. I got on my knees between her legs and I lifted one of her legs in the air. I don't remember if she was saying no or not. All I could hear was the pussy saying "please, please, please eat me."

I motioned for her to lie back on the bed. Her legs were on my shoulder. I dove in gladly. She had her hands on my head and was squeezing it tight. I wondered if this is what she wanted all along and was too reserved to entertain her curiosity. She was shaking so much, I had to look up to see if she was okay. I was trying to stop, but she kept my head in position. She started getting freaky and yelling at me.

"Don't stop!" she said. "You wanted to eat this pussy for a long time so eat it."

She shouldn't have said that. I ate her pussy like it was the last pussy in the world next to mine. I thought she would need a straight-jacket to keep her from shaking so much. She finally had an orgasm, but I could tell she wanted me to keep going by the way she kept moving around on the bed.

Since then, Sam and I never mentioned our little moment together. She has never been with another woman since then either. At least that's what I thought until I came to visit. Sam and I finally had an opportunity to have a girls-only weekend together and I was looking forward to it. We both thought we needed some rest and relaxation. She had been divorced now four years and was raising her children on her own. It was my first weekend without my studband and the kids.

I arrived at Sam's house and rung the doorbell several times. I tried knocking on the door as hard as I could to get her attention. I knew she was home because I just called about an hour earlier to let her know I was close by. My hands were full of bags. I forgot to get the key she mailed me two weeks ago out of my purse. After knocking and getting no answer, I finally put my luggage down and got the key out of my purse and unlocked the door.

I heard music blasting in the house. I was mad as hell that she didn't come to help me out. I was surprised by the look of the house. Sam was a single mother of three young children, but you couldn't tell kids even live here. I could tell she used my favorite aroma, Mango Febreeze. Suddenly, I heard one of my favorite songs, Monica's "Why I Love You So Much." Damn, the music was loud.

I yelled for Sam from the foyer to let her know I was there. It was no use. I headed upstairs to put my things down in the first bedroom on the right. She told me that was my room on the phone. I went to the bathroom in the bedroom and was amazed at how nice it was decorated. Damn! For a person who worked in the medical billing field, this bitch's house was off the chain.

I freshened up and got comfortable in a pair of shorts and a tank top. I sprayed some of my Forbidden Fantasy by Victoria's Secret all over me. One of my homegirls turned me on to that shit on a trip to the Tennessee Cabins. I was about to get in the bed to read the new Zane book I bought at the airport. I figured Sam was occupied and that's why the music was so loud. As I was about to flip the first page, I heard a faint moan between songs. It was like the first moan a woman makes when she gets that first lick on her pussy from another woman.

Curiosity got the best of me. I got out of bed and started to walk down the hall. I noticed one of the bedroom doors was slightly opened. The music was coming from inside. I walked up to the door, peeked inside, and I couldn't believe my eyes. I saw two women. I haven't seen my homegirl in a while so I wasn't sure if one of the women was Sam. I didn't care. My ultimate weakness was seeing two femmes have sex and this moment gave me a rush.

Then it hit me. Sam had been telling me about a surprise she had for me when I got to her house. If this was it, it was right up my alley.

However, I wouldn't have imagined Sam doing anything like this.

They changed positions. I backed out the doorway so I couldn't be seen. I slowly opened the door just a little more with my foot to get a better view. I damn near choked when I saw that it was my homegirl getting her freak on. I knew it was Sam by the tattoo of the sun on her stomach. Sam always wore shirts that showed her stomach so the tattoo was easy to see. That bitch was on top of another woman grinding her. Damn, she had to have been doing this for a long time before today. She looked like a pro.

They changed positions again. The woman on top of Sam had a nice body, too, and a tattoo in the middle of her back right above her ass. It looked like it said "can you handle it?" She had medium length dark hair and her skin was very dark. It was shining like she had been recently rubbed with baby oil. The two of them were sliding up and down on the bed. Their moans were getting louder, deeper, and heavier, as if it wouldn't be long before they both reached the ultimate orgasm.

I felt my panties getting wetter by the second and my nipples were dangerously hard. Damn, they changed positions again. Sam was on the bottom and was still in control. They were taking turns sucking each other's breasts. The other woman's sweat caused her hair to be stuck to her neck. They were still breathing loudly and out of control. She was riding Sam with such a stroke that it was as if she had been paid to do it. They looked like the letter X as they were poised for some serious clit to clit action. Honestly, that doesn't work for a plus size woman, but damn, I might try it the way they looked doing it.

Suddenly, I saw Sam lift this sexy woman up. While sucking her breasts, Sam slid two fingers inside the mystery woman's pussy. As their bodies shook together with excitement, I couldn't believe what I was seeing. I could tell they were about to climax. I didn't think I could stand there and watch another minute, but I couldn't move my feet either. They were glued to the plush carpet. I had no plans of heading back to my bedroom. This was too good.

I kept watching and before I knew it, my hand traveled down the front of my pants. Sam and the mystery woman moaned louder. I then heard the music switch to Sons of Funk's "Pushing Inside of You."

"Oh baby!" the mystery woman screamed.

"I'm cumming," Sam screamed.

At that moment, all I heard was a chorus of ahs and ohs. They finally climaxed, but shit, I didn't even get mine. I ran back to my room before they could notice me standing there or even hear me becoming more and more aroused.

I got in the bed like nothing happened. Sam had some serious explaining to do. I had all intentions of choking her ass when she came out the room. I was horny as hell and was in a city where I didn't know anyone except Sam. She was sexually satisfied, but I wasn't at that point just yet. But, I had Seimon, my vibrator, and Augustus, my strap-on. They'd make things all right.

She Finally Let Me Have a
Femme All to Myself

Have you ever just wanted to eat some pussy? I have and my girl finally let me have a femme all to myself right there in front of her. She sat back and got comfortable in her brown leather Lazy Boy chair and watched us as if she was watching her favorite movie in hi def. Just the thought of her looking at me having sex with a beautiful woman turned me on even more. All I wanted to do was show her what I could do.

The beautiful addition to our fantasy wanted it, too. I wanted to dive in right then. Traditional foreplay and sappy greetings were out of the question. Her pussy was so pretty. Her hair was cut low just the way I liked it. I just kissed it at first. Her clit was saying "hello" from the very first lick of my tongue. However, I wanted to admire it for a while longer, but I couldn't help it. Those caramel colored, thick thighs covered my ears, making all the sounds around me seem far away and muffled. Her repeated moaning was confirmation that I was licking her in just the right spot and that my tongue was her best friend in the world.

Tasting her was a great relief and comfort to me. I felt like I had just been released from a maximum security prison and her pussy was the only thing I craved, the only thing that made freedom more enjoyable. She tasted so damn good.

She raised her legs up higher so I put her whole pussy in my mouth. She arched her back. To drive her crazy, I just indulged in her wetness like an alcoholic until she couldn't take it anymore. But that was just the first of many orgasms to come.

Her body moved even more. It seemed like she was trying to escape from me, but I wouldn't let it happen. I wanted to eat her from the front to the back over and over and over again. I wanted the sweet smell of her all over my face. I never thought femme on femme sex would be like this.

My studband was still sitting in the corner just watching us go at it. I could tell she wanted to come over and join us. I knew the longer she watched, the more she was going to want me. I felt she was going to tear me up when she got to me. I knew she wanted to have both of us and we wanted her, too. But, for some reason, she didn't move. She just sat there and watched while biting her bottom lip.

"Oh, it feels so good," the femme screamed. She moaned loudly. She let me do what I wanted to do to her. I could be as aggressive as I wanted and even if she didn't agree, she never let me know she didn't like anything I tried. I grabbed her size breasts and then squeezed her large nipples like there was no tomorrow. I put the vibrator between my legs and I kept eating her like crazy.

My studband just sat there and watched. It must have been a dream. No stud I knew would sit there and watch while two beautiful women had sex, beckoning her to join in, too. If it was a dream, that's fucked up.

SHE FOOLED ME

I met her at school and at that time, she was so homophobic. That's what she said to me when she found out I was gay. When I asked her if she was a lesbian, she quickly uttered no. My gaydar was never wrong. I could recognize a stud in training when I saw one. She tried to make it seem like she always dressed as a boy because she didn't like dresses. But I knew it was much more than that. I should have known she was at least curious because she gave me her number and asked for mine. We didn't need partners for our lab work in class so why invite me over to her house so quickly?

She said that she was not gay and had no interest in women. For some reason, I felt she was lying and so I played on it. If she wasn't interested in women, why was she looking at me all the time in class? She simply replied that I was "an interesting woman." So, I asked if I could be her partner for the big class project at the end of the semester. She agreed. All I could think about was getting to her house. I figured I had what it took to bring the gay out of her. Unfortunately, she didn't call. I was disappointed, thinking that for the first time, my gaydar was wrong.

The teacher asked a group of us to stay after class for information about the final class project. She and I were among the few who had to stay. I looked at her, still wondering if I was actually wrong about her and that my gaydar just needed a tune-up. Perhaps she did manage to fool my intuition. Curiosity got the best of me as we waited for the professor to collect his thoughts and shuffle through the papers on his desk.

"Why didn't you call?"

"I did call."

I wasn't too shocked. I knew it. That whole speech about her just being tomboyish and liking guy clothes was just a cover up. If she wasn't gay, why did she even call? Then again, I didn't get any missed call messages on my phone so what kind of game was she playing?

"What are you going to do," I asked after the brief meeting with the professor was over.

"I'm going home."

"Can I go with you? It looks like we need to work out some details for this assignment since we're going to have to work together."

When we got to her house, we put our books on the kitchen table and started brainstorming about what needed to be done. Suddenly, she told me she hadn't had sex in eight months because her spouse went back home to Texas for whatever reason. She said that she was faithful.

"Awww," I said as if I really was interested. I knew what my goal was at the time. Inside, I was jumping up and down thinking this was the perfect opportunity. After all, she hasn't had sex with a woman and it had been a while since any action at all took place in her house.

I moved closer to her. She smiled and then she let me kiss her. Surprisingly, she actually kissed me back. The kissing turned intense and before long, we both had deep red passion marks on our neck. She quickly unhooked my bra, lifted my t-shirt, and sucked my nipples. I did the same to her.

"We can't go any further," she said as she kept my hand from continuing its journey along her side and stomach.

Naturally, I got pissed. I was all ready to turn her out and give her what she'd been missing for a long time. The flow was going strong, but I respected what she said. We hugged, said good bye, and then I left. When I got in my car, I was still excited. I pulled up my shirt and took my emergency travel vibrator out of the glove compartment. I sat there in the driveway and masturbated. I couldn't help myself. She got me all worked up then had the audacity to say, in not so many words, "not tonight." A part of me hoped that she would peek through the blinds and see what was happening. Maybe she did, but I was too focused on what was happening right there in the driver's seat.

I was mad as hell that we didn't go all the way. For the next few days, I didn't answer the phone whenever she called me. It got to the point that I could no longer avoid her calls. One day, I answered. She asked me to come over to discuss the project. Of course I didn't really believe her, but it was almost time to turn in the project outline and thesis.

It was 7 o'clock at night. I decided to go just in case she really did want to be studious.

As soon as I got there, she was throwing me all over the room. She kept kissing me, biting me, and sucking me on my neck. She suddenly lifted my skirt and began fingering me. I hate that shit normally, but she did it and I had an orgasm after orgasm. I was so confused. She said she had never been with a woman before. It felt like she had been lying to me all the while. But, I also loved it because she was doing everything like an aggressive, strapping stud. It was the way I liked it. The only bad part was she didn't have a strap-on.

How did she know where to kiss me and how to kiss me? I knew she was lying. After all the orgasms were over and me trying to figure her out, I gave up and went to use the bathroom. I yelled to her for a towel to freshen up with.

"Look under the sink," she said.

I opened the little cabinet door, my hands still wet. To my surprise, I saw a whole bag of what appeared to be strap-ons. At first, I was pissed because that was confirmation that she had been lying to me about being with another woman. Then, my anger turned into disgust. The strap-ons were all white and small, less than eight inches. I wanted to kick her ass for lying to me. I was also more and more interested in what she could really do with them. I retrieved the bag and headed back to the bedroom. She seemed shocked that I found it at all. Who could miss it? It was right in front.

"If you've never been with women, how the hell do you explain these strap-ons and all this Anal Ease and shit?"

"I haven't fucked any women," she insisted. "I fuck married men and I get paid for it.

"That's bullshit," I said. I found myself getting more and more disgusted. Suddenly, my interest in what she could do with the strap-ons turned into disappointment. I tossed the bag on the bed and stormed out the front door. As I got in the car, I noticed her peeking out the blinds.

"Too late for that shit," I said out loud to myself. She really fooled me.

Family Night

I always looked forward to family night. Last night, my baby, K.C., my children, and I had our normal family night of fun. It was the one night of the week when the whole family was together. Our schedules crossed a thousand ways and it was almost impossible to have a decent conversation with anyone longer than ten minutes. On family night, however, the rules were simple - no visitors, no one can get on the computer for any reason, and all cell phones must be turned off. My daughter called earlier in the day to say that she and K.C. had started dinner together and to my surprise, even the boys helped. It seemed everybody looked forward to family night. I loved it!

I stopped by the Quick Trip on my way home to buy my baby a box of Kamikaze flavored blunts and the kids some barbeque flavored Lays chips and a 2-liter Pepsi to have after dinner while we watched a movie. I was so happy that my professor cancelled class. I wanted to see *America's Next Top Model.* I had hoped that chic Jade would be asked to leave. However, K.C. and the kids wanted to see the *Hip Hop Awards Show.* I did, too, I suppose especially since it was in A-town. Our family watched anything about Atlanta.

It was K.C.'s night off and she wanted to cook for me. Damn I never imagined experiencing something like that in my previous relationships. No one wanted to cook for me, but they were all excited about sitting down to the table to eat anything I cooked. Damn, I loved me some K.C. Not only was she fine as hell, she could cook, too.

K.C. cooked fried, boneless chicken breasts, macaroni and cheese, and green beans. It was the thought that counted because in my mind, green beans didn't quite fit in with a meal like that. Just like a stud. My oldest son got involved by making some sweet, like-I–like-it Kool-Aid in the tropical punch flavor. That was my favorite.

When I finally got home, K.C. greeted me at the door with a big, strong hug and a tantalizing kiss.

"Meat!" she said as she took the shopping bags from my hand and casually dropped them on the floor next to my feet.

K.C. stole the nickname, "Meat," which was tattooed on an old friend of mine's father. It was located on his arm and boldly stood out from the others he wore proudly on his forearm and wrist. Ever since then, she called me that. I affectionately called her "Will," pretending she was Will Smith and I was Jada Pinkett.

"Hey Meat!" she said and kissed me in her normal cool ass way. I smiled as usual.

"Hey Will."

I caught a quick whiff of dinner and my eyes opened wide. I was so happy that my little Will decided to cook for me. I ran upstairs to shower and to put on a pair of her DKNY boxers and a black wife-beater. Her clothes were so comfortable to me. I could just lose myself in her clothes and get carried away by the scent of her favorite cologne, Bora Bora, that lingered in them even after they were washed. I melted whenever she was near me because that scent smelled so damn good on her. I grabbed the cover off the bed before heading back downstairs to begin what would be a very interesting family night.

K.C. and the kids tried to make everything so perfect. I tried to hold it back, but I had to laugh because it was so cute to me. They made sure I didn't raise a finger to do anything. I was forced to wait patiently for my dinner which my baby prepared for me. My youngest son, AJ, finally brought my food to me and I snickered at how everything was situated on the plate. I must admit, it was the little things that meant so much to me.

We sat down to watch *America's Next Top Model*. Everybody was eating, talking, and laughing. I, on the other hand, screamed the loudest when I saw those models doing their sexy walks on the runway. I kept flipping the channels on the remote so I wouldn't miss the Awards show or the latest cat-fight between the models. I almost lost my voice by the end of the awards show. T.I., Jay Z, and Busta were on the same show. That was hot!

Everybody had eaten and were full as hell. The meal was great. Eventually, the kids fell to sleep one by one. K.C. noticed all the closed eyes and loud snoring sounds coming from them and told them to go to their rooms. She followed them upstairs so I thought I'd be by myself watching TV the rest of the night. That was cool with me.

Besides, *Law and Order: SVU* was on and I loved that show, too.

K.C. came back downstairs and sat next to me. Her body was so warm next to mine. A mere touch from her was enough to give me goose bumps all over my body. I could just fall to sleep on her chest and never wake up until the next day. I wanted to kiss her, but I didn't want to give her just any kiss. I wanted to kiss her so hard. I wanted to give her the type of kiss that people usually reserve for those moments when people feel they'll never see each other again. I wanted to suck her bottom lip until I had that slight taste of the kamikaze blunt she smoked earlier on my lips. She must have read my mind.

"Do you want to play the peppermint game?" K.C. asked as I continued to stare at her lips. Of course, I wanted to play.

The peppermint game was a game we made up on our trip to Myrtle Beach. My favorite kind of peppermint was Bob's Peppermint because they were so soft and they literally melted in your mouth. First, she put the peppermint in her mouth and then we kissed and kissed and kissed until the peppermint moved from her month to mine. We continued to kiss until the peppermint was gone. There were no rules, except we couldn't bite it. Damn, by the time we finished the first peppermint, I was breathing hard. I wanted to go for round two, but I didn't want to seem greedy. We did it again anyway. We moved the peppermint in and out of our mouth and we were both totally into it.

She touched me. First, she grabbed my pussy just hard enough to let me know she was the boss. It was just enough for me to be turned on. I was so wet and I knew she felt it. I knew it was on when I felt her moving her hand down closer to my waterfall of love. I opened my legs wide enough so she could get those two fingers that she uses so well in the spot she wanted them to be in and in the place I yearned for her to be.

Just when I thought she was going to stimulate my clit with her fingers, I suddenly felt a vibration against my clit. She must have grabbed my vibrator when she went upstairs. She placed it on my clit at top speed. I couldn't even speak. My heart felt like it was going to come out my chest. I kept kissing her. The peppermint was so small. It was bound to disappear at any moment.

"Damn," I screamed out loud. I sucked her bottom lip so hard that even I was getting a hard on. "Shit," I yelled. She was still holding the vibrator on my clit. I didn't think I could take any more. I wanted to scream and she must have known that because she quickly grabbed the remote and turned up the volume on the TV. All I could hear was Detective Benson in the background reading somebody his rights and that strange music that plays when *Law and Order* was about to go off. I grabbed the cover and eventually I let her lip go.

"K.C., K.C. please," I said. She turned the vibrator down to a slower speed and whispered in my ear that she loved me.

"I want to be with you and tonight is all about you," she said as she softly nibbled on my

ear. She started to breathe more heavily. I wanted
her to turn the vibrator back up to full speed. She
knew.

"Relax," she said. "Be quiet and enjoy."

I willingly submitted to her demand. I
leaned back and she turned the speed up once
again. My heart was pounding. I wanted to release
my wetness all over her. I wanted this to last
forever. I wondered how she knew my body like
this. Before I knew it, my feet were balled up and
my legs were raised straight in the air. I screamed.

"Yes, yes, yes," I screamed at the top of my
lungs as I grabbed the back of her head and rubbed
her hair. She liked that and so did I.

"Here it is baaaaabyyyyy. I'm
cccccuuuuummmmmmiiiinnnngggg," I yelled out in
excitement as I gasped for breath.

Damn, that was wonderful. I actually had
tears in my eyes because for the first time, I had
experienced real intimacy. I wanted to give her
more. She made me feel so good. I was drained. I
couldn't even make it upstairs to go to my bed. I
hoped that was something I would experience again
and again.

Nobody's Really Faithful

I finally decided on the perfect anniversary surprise for my studband, CJ. She was a great spouse and wonderful with the kids. She worked third shift so it was easy to start planning for her, which meant I didn't really have to explain my whereabouts. I laid out her favorite white wife beater, Calvin Klein boxers, and house shoes. This was just a part of my normal routine. Although some of my friends didn't agree, I believed strongly in the old cliché "where one won't, one will." An old friend reminded me of that one a long time ago. I took that advice and ran with it.

My baby was an excellent provider, especially for her to be nine years younger than I am. I've been an out and proud lesbian for twelve years and I've had some good sex with some of my previous partners. But hands down, she was the best. Her sex knocked out competition from any man or woman I ever dated. We have tried it all! Just the thought of one of our love making scenes was enough to make me have a mental orgasm.

So yes, I handled my business in every way possible. I did it all from giving her massages, preparing her lunch for work, and making sure there was a hot meal on the table for dinner to washing and folding her clothes. I worked that ass out in the bedroom even when I didn't want to do some of the wild shit she wanted to do. I did it anyway because "where one won't, one will."

My homegirls were all like "bitch, please. I am not doing all that." That would explain why their woman complained about their sorry asses, came home late, and why they felt sexually neglected. I didn't worry my baby with silly questions like "where have you been, where are you going, or when are you coming back?" All the nagging was unnecessary. To me, that drove your mate away from you and into the arms of other women. If you were really handling your business, and doing it well, she would never leave.

I talked to many couples. They told me about all the areas in which their women lacked. Therefore, I used some of them as a model of do's and don'ts in my own relationship. I must say thanks to all of the women in the submissive role because I avoided some of the mistakes you have made in your relationships. My relationship was afloat. It wasn't perfect. We got mad at each other like any other couple, but never to the point where we betrayed each other's trust.

Most of you are too comfortable to leave a relationship that you know you are not happy being in. I have been down that road before. CJ and I were past that shit. We have our ways of venting. In a relationship, you are both human so shit happens. Before you can check anyone, you have to check yourself. I knew she was the one for me. When she touched me, goose bumps instantly covered my body. I wanted her, not just sexually, but I want her mentally and physically.

Anyway, back to the anniversary surprise. I was sure that it was perfect for her. I had been going to all the swingers clubs in the area looking for the perfect present. But this place was my last option and my final hope. It was an all women swingers club! My baby and I had been talking about having a threesome for about two years. So, for our anniversary this year, my plan was to see if she was just talk or if she really wanted to do it.

I wanted us to have a threesome. Call me crazy, but I wanted to see how we were with a third person. In addition, I was a Cancer and so was she. Cancers generally don't recognize limits. They will try anything and they love anything that's sexy. I mean damn, our zodiac sign was a 69. I just wanted to get my freak on even though sometimes I acted like I didn't want to. I heard it was every true stud's fantasy to be intimate with two femmes at the same time. My baby deserved this treat. I put the final touches on my makeup, grabbed my keys, and headed out the door.

As I turned into the parking lot, I had to slowly make my way through the maze of BMWs, Envoys, Benzes, and Lexus cars and trucks. My dream car, the Cadillac CTS, was parked toward the front of the lot. It was in full gear, complete with a set of 22-inch rims, dark tinted windows, and a recently detailed shine that made it stand out from the rest of the cars. I couldn't believe these cars were on the southside of town. Everybody knew the southside was supposedly the worse place to be in any city in Georgia, but it was the best place to party, too. I suppose everybody had a little hood in them.

I walked toward the front door, my I.D. in hand and ready to meet the lucky lady who'd join my baby and me for some adult fun. As I walked, I couldn't help but notice the club's awkward appearance. The building looked abandoned. It was dark in some areas of the parking lot and the other lights blinked as if they were going to go out at any minute. All the times that I've passed by this place, I thought it was an empty warehouse. I was hesitant to go in, but I had to follow through with it any way. As I made my way through the parking lot, I read the sign on the door: "Welcome to Heaven."

There was a long line of women waiting to get in. I moved forward and took one last look at my appearance to make sure I looked good and smelled good. My hair was freshly braided, courtesy of Mama's Hair Braiding on Campbellton Road in the SWATS. I wore a sexy v-neck black and gray shirt with my 48 triple D's sitting at attention and waiting to be admired. I had on a gray skirt with some footless tights and a pair of black 4-inch stilettos by Carol Santana. I sprayed the last of my Christian Dior's *J'adore* in all the right spots on my body.

As I waited at the end of the line to get in, three women walked up behind me and took their places at the end of the line. They were talking about what happened at their job earlier in the day. From their conversation, it seemed they were all nurses. That's when I saw the security guard.

She was about six foot four inches tall. She was patting the women down and checking for identification and weapons. She seemed to have had a very cocky demeanor, but from top to bottom, she looked perfect. She had on a pair of black Enyce jeans, a black T-shirt that read, "Security," a security belt with a 9mm gun on her right side, and a billy club on the left. I could tell that she was binding, a process some studs go through to make their breasts look much smaller and similar to a guy's chest using Ace bandages and the like. Normally I don't like that, but she pulled it off very well. Her hair was cut in a low fade style with tiny designs on the side. Her pants were baggy, but not baggy enough. I still noticed every inch of that nine inch, three fingers wide strap-on. Yes, I can measure a strap-on with my eyes. Her nametag read, "TROUBLE."

I could tell she was very cocky as she stood there like she knew that she is the shit. I must admit, however, I loved that shit. "Damn," I thought. Something said I should have left right then. Besides a clean, wet, shaved pussy and watching two femmes making passionate love, seeing a strapping stud in public was definitely one of my weaknesses. That's just what I like. I had to prepare myself just for walking up to her. Get it together, girl, I thought to myself. I was here for CJ. But, shit! I could look at the menu and admire all of the tasty stud entrees.

It was finally my turn. She motioned for me to step forward and began to check me for weapons. It felt like she was patting each of my legs with her beautiful lips. I was in my own little part of Heaven. In my mind, all I could say was, "yes, yes, yes." Each pat felt like she was caressing my body with an intensity I've never felt before.

"Ma," she said.

I guess I didn't hear her because I was dreaming about those sexy lips of hers taking a journey up and down my legs.

"Ma," she said again.

She caught me off guard this time.

"Yes?"

I quickly snapped out of my dream. Damn, the fun is over already.

"Fill your ticket out and put it in the box," she said as I continued to look at her. I wanted to tell her that she could check me anytime. As a matter of fact, I'm going to whisper in her ear that I have a blade in my panties the next time I come to the club. I know. I'm bad. That, among other things was why my baby loved me. I wasn't like most women in relationships. I'd try anything once. There was no limit to what I would do.

I answered the questions on my ticket and put it in the box. "What's your fantasy?" and "Would you like to fulfill it tonight?" These were just two of the bold questions on the ticket. I took one more look at Trouble and headed inside the club to complete my mission. Normally I would be tripping about the cover charge, but just from the look of the club on the inside and the jolt I got from Trouble patting me down at the door, the $35.00 cover charge was well worth it. When I walked in the club, I saw what appeared to be a huge dance floor. After a closer look, it was actually a make-out floor. The women looked like they were making love right there in the middle of the floor. They were definitely moving to their own special groove.

To my right was a huge stage with large curtains like the kind you would see in a school auditorium. The curtains were partially opened. All I could see was a little refrigerator and a bottle of Arbor Mist on the table with three glasses. The DJ booth was to my left. Five women were standing in line waiting to request a song. I looked a little closer. Damn! Was I crazy or was that Trouble's fine ass acting as the DJ, too. I was so shocked at how much the DJ and Trouble looked alike. I had to walk back toward the entrance. With great satisfaction, I noticed there were two of them. I had to say a silent prayer to myself because Trouble and the DJ made me sin a million times just thinking about what could happen between the three of us. Now that was Heaven. I wasn't sure if she was strapping. However, the two of them still turned me on. My mind was going a thousand different ways. I was definitely going to request a song or two and tip her fine ass.

As I walked back into the club, a waitress assured me that Pain, the DJ's name, and Trouble were twins. I guess she could see how much I was tripping just by the way I smiled at Trouble and how quickly I tried to make it back toward the DJ booth. My, my, my, my, my! It was on. I sat at an empty table that was close to the stage and the DJ booth. I noticed there was a bed on the stage. If someone was going to get in it, I'd be the first to see what happened up close and personal.

For some reason, I felt like prey as I looked around the club. Almost everybody was looking at me. I wondered why. I knew that I had Beauti and Ful sitting pretty underneath my shirt, but they were looking at me as if they wanted one in their mouth. Shit, I was thinking that something could be arranged to satisfy their curiosity. I noticed one couple still checking me out. I thought I would put on a show just for them. I asked the server to bring me a sex on the beach with extra cherries. I positioned the chair so both of them could have a full view of me. I wanted to take Augustus, the name I affectionately call my vibrator, out of my purse, pull my panties to the side, and masturbate in front of them.

Instead, I crossed my legs. The server, whose name was Pleasure, only wore an apron as she quickly came back with my drink. Now I can't drink a lick, but shit, I felt like coming out of my norm. Drinking a sex on the beach was as about as brave as I could be when drinking by myself. I could never drink a Long Island Iced Tea or a Blue Motherfucker. I looked at Pleasure, thanked her for her service, and gave her a generous tip. At that moment, I knew my baby would love Club Heaven.

"Can I ask you a question?" Pleasure asked after she thanked me for the tip.

"You just did," I said to her sarcastically. We both laughed momentarily. Suddenly, she popped the question.

"Do you want to fulfill your fantasy tonight?"

"I'd love to," I responded as I thought back to the ticket that Trouble asked me to fill out when I entered the club. Although I wrote my fantasy was for me to have a threesome with two femmes with toys and no limits, my real fantasy was to have two strapping studs make some very aggressive hair pulling, bitch calling, ass spanking, strap sucking S&M sex with me. However, I couldn't write that on the paper.

Pleasure assured me that someone would come and get me when the time was right. As she walked off, I noticed I still had an audience. I picked up my drink, got the first cherry out, and ate it very seductively. Then, I tied the stem in a bow with my tongue. I did the same with the next cherry.

Then "she" walked by. I didn't know her name, but if I had to give her one, it would be Desire. She was everything I liked in a woman. She was thick, she smelled good, and she worked the hell out of those black heels she was wearing. She would be the perfect anniversary surprise because she was the kind of woman my baby liked. She could be my woman, too. Then again, there was only one bitch in my house and that was me. I wished that we could become acquainted, though.

I watched her walk from one end of the club to another. She had a nice ass. She could be at one end of the club and her ass would be at the other end. She was a beautiful, plus size, mocha colored woman who appeared to be in her mid 20s. Her body was really shaped like a coke bottle. She had that sexy ass Marilyn Monroe piercing above her top lip on the right side. She didn't have on any make-up, but she had some shiny ass lips.

Shit, she started walking this way. If she was bold enough to say something to me, then she would definitely be the one I need for my big anniversary surprise. Damn, I loved an aggressive femme. As she moved closer to me, I couldn't help but pray that she was a lesbian. My prayer was interrupted when I heard Pain's sexy ass voice over the loudspeaker.

"Fantasy and Sin-sation to the stage, please," Pain said.

I saw people pointing to a woman walking toward me. It was Fantasy. She walked right by me, so close that I could tell what kind of perfume she had on. She had on some Forbidden Fantasy perfume by Victoria Secret and she smelled great. She finally disappeared into the back behind the stage. I didn't know who Sin-sation was because for some reason, everyone was moving from the back to the front of the club near the stage. While all the commotion was going on, I heard Pain request Fantasy and Sin-Sation at the DJ booth. Then some chic came out of the door close to the stage area where Fantasy went. She ran to the DJ booth, whispered something to Pain, and then Pain spoke again.

"Ladies and gentlewomen," Pain said. "I hope you have your drinks and have already been to the restroom because you might wet your pants and die of thirst while watching Sin-sation and Fantasy on stage."

The curtains opened, the lights dimmed, and the crowd became gradually quiet. Floetry's "Say Yes" played. I loved that song. It was the same track that my baby and I made passionate love to. Fantasy came to the stage. Fantasy's outfit changed, but the only way I knew it was her was that ass. Fantasy and Sin-sation were standing face to face on stage in what was designed to look like a small apartment. There was a black couch and a canopy bed with two large pillows and the covers pulled back. There was a small wooden table in the middle and a TV that appeared to be showing a lesbian porn movie.

Fantasy and Sin-sation pretended they were a couple having a dispute. Fantasy kept walking back and forth across the stage in frustration and anger.

Fantasy asked, "Am I not enough woman for you, Sin-sation?" Perhaps Fantasy feared that if they had someone come into their relationship sexually, that it may end their relationship.

I leaned over to this sexy ass stud sitting next to me and asked, "Shit are they acting because this looks real as hell."

She laughed. "Ma, I was thinking the same thing."

We both looked back on the stage. "You're either down or you aren't," Sin-sation said.

"Please, baby, don't go," replied Fantasy.

"I love you, baby, but you have to be open to new things."

They both stood there holding one another's hands and talking. Finally, Fantasy agreed. The music came back on louder and the curtains closed again. Suddenly, Adina Howard's "T Shirt and Panties" was the next sound we heard. Fantasy and Sin-sation talked about what would happen when they had the threesome. Pain lowered the music.

"Girlfriend to the stage," Pain said as her voice echoed in my ear, making me even more excited.

I looked around for the so-called girlfriend to come to the stage. Then I remembered what the waitress said to me. Hell no! I couldn't believe it. I noticed Pleasure standing at the bar. She started walking toward me. She motioned for me to go around the side of the stage and wait for her at the door. I stood up, shocked as hell, and really feeling my drink. "What am I doing?" I thought to myself. I continued to walk to the backstage area anyway.

When I got to the door, Pleasure was standing there. She briefed me on what my lines were.

"After your third line, just go with the flow," she insisted. She then grabbed my hand and escorted me up three steps and finally onstage. Fantasy greeted me.

"Hello," she said.

Sin-sation walked over to Fantasy who was sitting on the bed shaking her head.

"Baby, I love you. There is nothing I wouldn't do for you," Fantasy said in a low voice, yet still audible enough for the crowd to hear.

"I promise I'm not here to break up your relationship," I said to Fantasy, "but remember 'where one won't, one will.'" Oh shit, I actually acted out the scene. I surprised myself. I guess now was the time to just go with the flow.

"Okay," Fantasy said.

"Fantasy, I promise you will never forget this," Sin-Sation said in an excited tone.

Sin-sation walked over to the little refrigerator that I saw when I was in the crowd. She took out three glasses and grabbed the bottle of Arbor Mist. We drank and toasted to a new friendship. Sin-sation suddenly grabbed Fantasy and gave her a kiss. Then she grabbed me and put me in front of Fantasy. I just stood there thinking that the acting was over. I was horny.

Fantasy kissed me as if she had wanted to do it since I walked on the stage. Before I knew it, we were all over the staged apartment on the bed, table, and the couch. I was having sex with Fantasy and Sin-Sation. We were taking turns licking Fantasy and it drove her crazy. Sin-sation put her hand under the pillow and pulled out some interesting toys. There were also two strap-ons. Damn, I wanted to be the one to use one of them. Sin-sation sensed my desire to take control and gave me one of the strap-ons and she put on the other. I motioned for Fantasy to get up and I turned her over on her knees in front of me. She was so wet. One of my weaknesses was seeing a nice, wet pussy and her ass was so pretty.

I rubbed the strap-on up and down her wetness and she moved back toward me like she wanted it. Sin-sation laid in front of Fantasy. Fantasy started licking on Sin-sation's inner thigh.

That was turning me on. The moaning from both of them was so sexy, erotic, and all that freaky shit.

I entered Fantasy slowly. She moaned with excitement. She must have cum as soon as the strap-on entered her. The strap-on looked as if it had been dipped in baby oil. I continued to stroke her slowly. She started throwing the puss back at me. Before I knew it, I lost control. I didn't remember Sin-sation getting out of the bed or even changing positions. She began strapping me. I went over the rules in my head, which simply stated that you shouldn't look into their eyes, don't close your own eyes, and understand that it was just sex, nothing else. It didn't matter how good it felt.

I put Fantasy's right leg in the bend of my right arm and then I grab the head of the strap-on and rubbed it up and down her wetness. She was in heaven. She bit her bottom lip and began moaning. She wanted more. Her moan was music in my ears. I couldn't take it. I was past being turned on. Why was this happening? This was just supposed to be sex, not a long term commitment. Why did it feel so good? What about the rules? We were so connected-lips to lips, breast to beast, strap-on to her waterfall of love. My eyes were closed.

Our bodies were screaming in ecstasy. The only noise in the room was the heavy moaning and Adina's song, "Nasty Grind" playing in the background. I finally took the strap-on out of her and kissed and bit her neck, but not hard enough to break the skin. She grabbed me with all her might because she didn't want me to stop. Shit, I didn't

want to stop either. We had forgotten all about Sin-
sation. Before I knew it, I lost my mind in Fantasy.
She was talking dirty and saying "yes, yes, get this
pussy. I know you want it." Our moans were in
unison. All that could be heard was "oh yes, damn,
oh yes, damn."

Out of nowhere, someone called my name.
It sounded like a familiar voice. I slowed my pace
after entering and stroking Fantasy down once
again. But, I refused to stop just because I heard
my name. I turned and looked into the crowd.
Everything was going so well, I forgot I was in the
club. The crowd was looking at me in awe. They
wanted to see more and since I didn't see anyone
that I knew, I kept going and got back into the
groove. I noticed several ladies on the front row
who were looking with their legs crossed tightly.
The action on stage was turning them on. They sat
there in their seats squirming like crazy.
My legs were getting weak. I was about to cum.
Fantasy was about to cum, too.

"Oh, oh, oh, oh shit," we screamed. All of a
sudden, the music stopped and I heard CJ's
voice. I turned and saw her in the DJ booth. She
knocked Pain over and grabbed the microphone.
Everybody looked at her, including me. Her voice
was strong and full of hurt. She screamed my
name. I could tell she was pissed.

"Bitch, fuck you! I knew you was on some
bullshit," CJ yelled out from the DJ booth.
Everybody in the club was watching and waiting to
see what would happen next. I just wondered what
the fuck she was doing there and not at work.

You

Damn, I wished we had gotten dressed in different rooms that day, but we were in a hurry. We were both naked and I saw your entire body. Damn, you were sexy.

Since that day, I've been thinking about you all the time. It's gotten totally out of hand. I replay that day over and over and over again in my head. I've even masturbated looking at the picture of you on the beach in your red two-piece bathing suit relaxing on the sand as the ocean tickled your toes.

I've fallen in love with everything about you. I don't know if it was your pecan tanned skin, which was so soft when you hugged me. Maybe it was your beautifully styled afro that you kept naturally low. It could have been the perfectness of your breasts or your nipples, which to me, always seemed to be hard and pointing directly at me. Was it the sleek and sexy shape of your body? Maybe it was just that I loved to watch you walk across the room with a style and demeanor that said you could have anything you wanted. Perhaps it was just simply an insatiable craving I had for you. Whatever it was, something drew me closer and closer to you and I just couldn't resist you.

You smelled of sweet nectar. Even when you were dressed, my eyes envisioned you completely naked and vulnerable before me. And when you hugged me to say hello, you awakened my several senses and turned me on completely.

But you belong to another, one I can not betray. In my mind, however, I can imagine a sweet love that only you and I can share. It's a love in which you and I are completely happy, sharing many of life's golden moments and surprises. Alas, you're my brother's wife and my secret obsession. I can't have you in the way that he can. I can't hold you in the way that he can. I can't kiss you and make love to you in the way that he can. I can't touch your body and feel how it responds to me. All I can do is wish I was with you, dream of you, and look forward to the next family gathering. Then, will I be able to admire you and take comfort in everything that makes you, You.

Random Erotic Thoughts

H ave you ever just wanted to fuck?
I'm not talking about any of all that
foreplay shit. I'm talking about
straight fucking. I certainly have had my moments
when all I wanted was a good fuck. I recall one
moment, not long ago, and it started like this.

I had a hard ass day at work. The boss got
on my last nerve. My coworkers were all on their
cycles. At least that's how it seemed because they
all had an attitude. I was ready to get home. I
pulled into the driveway and there she was standing
at the door waiting for me. She smiled and I
smiled back. Damn, I wanted her so bad, but too
bad her ass had to go to work. Once I go
downstairs to fix her lunch, she'll be off to work
for a long 12 hours.

I had to do something. I wanted sex so bad,
I could feel the pressure building inside me,
waiting to explode in an instant. My pussy wasn't
tryin' to hear the bullshit about her going to work.
I wanted to fuck and "not right now, baby" was not
the right answer and was definitely not an option.

I ran upstairs to take a shower. After I
showered and put on some baby lotion, I sat there
on the bed thinking. What if I just put on a tight,
short skirt without panties and went to her job?
What if I rode shotgun with her and masturbated
while she drove to work? What if I showed up at
her job right at break time and demanded action?
Fuck it, I can't do that. I don't want her to get

fired, but I was really strategizing on how to overcome that overnight, gotta work shit. I put a dab of my Clinique perfume on my neck, shoulder, and wrists. That always drove her ass crazy. I rubbed it in my hands and across my pussy, too. I could've fucked myself at that moment, but it's not the same as having her inside me.

My pussy was so wet. I must have been horny as hell. Damn! That shit turned me on. I couldn't help myself. I rubbed my clit with such intensity that in just a few moments, I reached my breaking point. I was temporarily satisfied, but ultimate gratification could come only from her.

I sat there still thinking about her and how she holds me from the back when she walks up behind me. Then she would tell me how good I smelled and kiss my neck while grabbing my erect nipples. She could turn me on any time of the day.

Mentally, I was just saying to her "yes, yes, please fuck me." But, I didn't want just any kind of fuck. I wanted that fuck me hard, like your life depended on it kind of fuck. Or maybe that fuck me rough, like a gangster from the baddest neighborhood kind of shit. I could even go for the fuck me like you just got out of prison after ten years and a hot, wet pussy was all you wanted. I just wanted her to make me scream like a bitch.

Before my thoughts of the perfect, right now fuck were complete, she came upstairs to join me on the bed. She turned me around to face her. There she was before me in a pair of her Calvin Klein boxers, the ones I got her for Christmas.

"Why are you still here? Shouldn't you be getting ready for work," I asked, knowing that I didn't give a shit about a job at that moment.

Was I fucking nuts? I wanted her to stay, but I knew she had to go. All I could do was just simply look her up and down and imagine what could be going down in the next few minutes if I had my way. And then I saw it. She was wearing the "big boy."

She started kissing me and I became an instant river of delight. She then started to rub my pussy. I pulled that beautiful, black ten inches long and three fingers wide strap-on out of those boxers. Fuck work, I thought. She's about to get some serious overtime right now.

She continued to rub my wet pussy and then started biting my ear. With the deepest Brooklyn slang, she whispered in my ear.

"Why ya pussy so wet," she said. "Were you thinkin' 'bout me?"

I wanted to respond, but my breathing was too intense, I couldn't form even a single word. She was rubbing my pussy to the point I was almost about to cum hard.

"Yes, yes, baby," I screamed. "I'm about to cum, baby." Not yet. I wanted even more. I got down on my knees and took hold of her strap-on and sucked it. She always loved that shit. The way she was moaning, I thought she could really feel it. It may be just a mental thing with studs, but at that point, I didn't give a shit. As long as she got hers, I was happy. I could tell she was about to cum. I already came twice so I was just waiting for her. It finally happened.

I stood up. We kissed again. She then turned me around and bent me over the bed. My head was facing the headboard and my hands were on the bed. In one quick motion, she put one of my legs in the air, just slightly above the top of the bed while the other leg still rested on the floor. My head rested on the mattress. She began teasing me with the strap-on, gently rubbing it up and down my pussy. I wanted to scream, "fuck me!"

"You want this, don't you," she said. I couldn't help but wonder if she just simply read my mind and knew what the fuck I was thinking. I didn't know if she really wanted an answer, so I didn't say anything. She asked again.

"Yes, baby, please!"

"Are you begging for it?"

"Yes, shit, yes!"

She was extremely turned on and so was I. Before I knew it, she was inside me. I was so wet. She started out slowly, putting it in carefully, but I just simply wanted to fuck.

"Fuck me, fuck me," I shouted. "I don't want that weak ass shit. Fuck me harder, baby!"

All of a sudden, she started going crazy inside me. That was what I needed. I started throwing the pussy right back at her. She was off the chain in my pussy, fucking me the way I liked it, doggy style. It felt so good.

"Yes, baby, yes! Fuck me, fuck me," I said.

She reached over to grab the pair of red crotchless panties I was going to put on and then put them in my mouth. I couldn't speak. All I could do was let out incoherent screams. I couldn't fucking believe it. Even with this, I just knew the neighbors could hear what was going on. I felt my legs getting weak. I couldn't hold it much longer.

She then put her left hand on my left shoulder and with her right hand, grabbed and pulled my hair. The strap-on was so deep in my pussy that I didn't know what to think. I couldn't take it anymore. She thrusted harder and harder until I let out a scream that could have very well shook the whole neighborhood.

I gasped just enough air to let my her know that I couldn't hold it anymore.

"Baby, I'm cummming," I screamed as loud as I could through the panties she put in my mouth. I fell to the bed in both satisfaction and exhaustion. That was the feeling I wanted and she gave it to me. She kissed me on the forehead, said good bye, and left for work. I went to sleep. Before she left for work, she left a note on the bed. It simply read: *"Thanks for lunch. I look forward to breakfast."*

Make Up to Break Up

We each have tears in our eyes. Sweat is dripping all over our bodies. We are so close that we look like one person. We love each other so much. We're both in orgasm heaven and we're screaming so loud that anyone walking by could hear us and wonder what was happening. They could picture the passion we're experiencing as they walk by. They'd be able to hear every "yes, baby," "give it to me, baby," and "I want it, baby" cries.

The sex is beautiful as usual, but who are we fooling? We both know there isn't anything left between the two of us. We are just too comfortable to let go. What should we do to get out of this? We know we aren't in love with each other anymore. We just can't seem to let go.

It's true that people really do stay in relationships because they've become comfortable. And here we are, both of us too comfortable with one another to walk away. But, how should we end this? We aren't in love anymore.

We continually break up just to make up. I think I figured it out. It's the feeling of being wanted that we live on. That's truly what we strive for each time we are touching. We have both hurt each other before. We have cheated on each other. Why are we still together?

We'd look strange trying to get into the dating scene at our ages. We know that we don't handle rejection well at all and we know that we don't want to start over and begin teaching someone else our likes and dislikes. We don't want to learn theirs either.

But, how many times do we try to mentally and verbally kill each? This is so crazy. We continue to hurt each other just to fight, cry, and have sex. The make-up is what we live on, but there is not enough love left to keep us alive.

We love each other so much. We are both in orgasm heaven, screaming so loud that anyone walking by could hear us. Our moans are so intense that anyone who hears us could picture the passion just by listening. The question is, could they feel or hear the love that is between us? Probably not.

I Have a New Lover

Ⅰ am living today as if I only have this day to live. It's all because I have a new lover and she is me. I am finally in love with myself, so much so that I don't need anyone else, not even you. Why does it feel this way? Could it really be true that another can make my body, mind, and soul forget all about you?

At first, I refused to believe it. I still loved you more than anything. How is it possible? My body is supposed to respond to only you. All I can do is replay the love that we shared, the promises we made to be together, and the plans we made for our future together.

Because of you, the promises you made to stay with me forever, and all the things we went through, I didn't think I could ever let my guard down again. But, that's not fair. You see, I have learned that in life, nothing is promised to anyone. Anything could happen. We aren't promised tomorrow so it's best to either live life day by day or sit and worry about how tomorrow will turn out. I choose to live.

I wondered how could a person have your heart one minute and let it go so easily the next minute. I'll never have the answer to that and I don't even want the answer any more. You see, someone else wants my heart. She's been patiently waiting for you to fuck up. She always knew you would, but I would always defend you and say, "No, my baby loves me. She is here for the long haul." She would say that you don't seem to love me anymore, "Well If she is over you, why can't you be over her?"

My smile turned to a frown. I said to myself over and over again that I'll get over you. I've climbed higher mountains than this and you know that because many of them, you climbed with me. Maybe that's why you are so calm about it all, but one thing is for sure. No matter how much love and devotion I put into future relationships, because of you, I will always have a Plan B.

What I can't seem to understand is how one could be in love with you so deeply one week and the next week be so far from loving you. It's as if you never knew them.

The moral of this story is nothing is promised to you. If someone had told me I wouldn't be with the love of my life today, I wouldn't believe them. That's why I live for today because tomorrow is not promised.

So, if you see me and I appear to be a little wilder than you thought I should be, just know I'm living today like I only have this day to live. Since you left me, that's truly how I feel.

Everything Isn't What
It Appears to Be

When I first realized that I had an attraction for girls, I was in the eighth grade at Roberts Jr. High School in Waveland, Mississippi. It was in gym class, the one class I absolutely hated, but it was also the one place I was able to at least hang out with other girls. I wasn't popular in junior high at all. My mother was away in the army and I lived with my church-going grandmother. She didn't allow any socializing outside of church so unless a person rode the school bus with me or there was a church revival, I didn't see anyone outside of church.

Gym class was the one place where the big girls were teased the most. No one wanted to pick the big girl to be on their team. She might not run fast enough to win the 440 relay race or she might not jump high enough to hit the volleyball over the net. Although I loved volleyball, that was not the reason I damn near broke my neck running through the hallway as fast as I could to get to gym class. I could care less if anyone picked me, but I was always the first one in the dressing room.

Gym class was more exciting sitting on the bleachers and watching the girls' breasts go up and down each time they jumped for the volleyball. I would put my clothes on quickly so when the other girls got to the dressing room, I'd already be dressed and sitting there putting lotion on my legs.

They changed into their gym clothes right in front of me. Sadly, the only naked body I had ever seen was mine and my grandmother's. Eeeww! Oh my God! They were only junior high girls, but their bodies looked like full grown women. They had large perky breasts, wide hips, and big booties. They even wore thongs. My grandmother didn't buy me stuff like that. My panties covered my entire ass. Hell, they damn near covered my whole body. I hated being teased so much about wearing those big underwear or "granny panties" as some people call them now.

One day I bought my first pair of thongs. My grandmother and I went to Fred's Dollar Store for our weekly shopping trip. My mom sent me money because I made good grades last semester. My grandmother said I could go look in the clothing section and buy whatever I wanted. I wanted a pair of the black thongs with the tiny flower prints. I slipped to the front of the store, made my purchase, and asked the cashier to point me to the restroom. While my grandmother was still shopping and comparing prices on bleach and laundry detergents, I was planning to show the girls in gym the next day how a big girl wears thongs. By the time I got home, I realized that thongs were not for me. I didn't like them then and I still don't. For some reason, there were a lot of them still in my dresser. Just to commemorate all those hippy and busty girls in gym class, I would put on a pair every now and then.

I've been attracted to women almost all my life. There was never anything exciting about my experiences with a man. Besides, being with a man was more of a game for me. The strongest man could be broken down to a little boy by the power of some good pussy and if a woman has a combination of good pussy and good head, the man didn't have a chance. My last sexual encounter with a man was more than ten years ago. I can't lie. I've done it all. But, when I decided that I wouldn't have sex with a man again, I went to see a counselor.

I never told anyone about me going to a counselor until recently. It was my little secret. I really wanted to know why I was so interested in women and why men no longer aroused my curiosity. I didn't understand it. My family was middle class. My parents were both preachers. I never had to spend time at home alone because someone was always there every day. I had tons of positive role models, too. There were never any drugs or alcohol abuse. I went to church 24/7. At one point, I like men. Shit, I felt I loved one or two of them. Actually, I loved the sexual control I had over them. I just wanted answers and felt a counselor could tell me exactly why I was so attracted to women.

Two thousand dollars and 6 months later, I came up with my own conclusion. No one knew me like me. I refused to continue to pay a stranger to tell me about me and what I liked. I had to face the reality that I was a lesbian. Even during counseling, my feelings about women didn't change a bit. I said that I wouldn't see another counselor again, but I kept going for another five months. It wasn't because I was questioning my life as a lesbian. I was 100% sure that I wanted pussy and not dick and I was definitely happy about my relationship. Shun and I had been together now for three years. She was so good to me, everything I would ever want in a woman. For the most part, we had a beautiful relationship. I was happy for once and have actually been faithful to her. However, six months ago, I started cheating on Shun with Tina. Tina and I started seeing each other in late October 2006, but our relationship started to get out of hand. It was affecting my work performance, and that was something I couldn't allow because I really loved my job.

It all started when I was in the bathroom at work. I was doing the normal check of my clothes and touching up my lip-gloss. That's about all I had to do because true beauty didn't need many adjustments. I washed my hands, shook the excess water off, and reached for a paper towel. I looked up to check my sexy full figure frame once more before leaving. I noticed that she was standing there near the other of the restroom. She startled me because I didn't hear the door open and I thought I was alone.

"You caught me off guard," I said to her.

"That's not bad all the time," she responded.

I didn't quite understand what she meant, but I said hello to her anyway. "My name is Denise," I said to her as I finished drying my hands and tossed the paper towels into the trash. I smiled and shook her hand.

"I'm Tina. I'm new here."

"Are you new to the call center or just new to our wonderful city?"

"Both," Tina said. "Denise, are you always this cheerful?"

"I just smile a lot because I don't feel everyone should know if you're having a bad day. Sometimes people can make something out of nothing. I learned that a long time ago. Not everybody will be interested anyway."

We both laughed.

"Denise, I like you. We have to talk again," she said with a very devilish smile.

"That's cool," I agreed.

I didn't know what happened to her because I didn't see her for another week or so. The next time I saw her, I was on my lunch break at Walmart getting some snacks to take back to my desk. I stopped to use the restroom just to wet my face because for some reason, I was having some serious hot flashes. I washed my face in cold water, reached for a towel, dried off, and looked up in the mirror to check my makeup.

Tina was in front of the sink in the mirror saying she had to use the bathroom. She was jumping up and down in a frenzy with both of her hands behind her back reaching for the zipper. She asked me to help her. I laughed at the spectacle she was making of herself and reached over to help unsnag her zipper. I didn't want to get too close to her. It seemed strange to unsnag a zipper for a woman I've only had conversations with in the restroom. After two attempts to help, I stopped.

"Girl, how long have you been in here jumping up and down like this?"

"Not that long," she said.

Somehow, I just knew that by then she knew I was a lesbian. I wasn't shy about it, but something made me ask if she really knew. I believed in the power of gaydar, but rarely did I show up on anyone's map, even the more seasoned lesbians. It just happened that way. I was subtle.

"Yes," she said. "Denise, word travels fast around here."

I couldn't say anything. My mind went blank. Everybody knew? What did I do to give myself away, I thought.

"Denise, we are in Walmart. I won't try anything unless you want me to."

I was shocked as hell. She was finally able to unzip her pants and ran into the stall. After she finished her business, she came out, washed her hands, and stood there in front of me as she placed her hands under the mega dryer on the wall.

"Girl, I know family when I see them," Tina said.

"What do you mean?"

"Denise, where you want to say you're gay or you live an alternative lifestyle, it doesn't matter. I know a lesbian when I see one." Tina continued with her speech on lesbianism like she was a pro in the whole matter.

Like a kid on Christmas, I was excited for some strange reason.

"Tina," I asked. "Are you a lesbian?"

"Ssshhh," she said in a quiet voice.

I apologized for my excitement. There weren't a lot of us around town and at work. I looked at my watch and noticed that time was going by fast. I had to get back to the office. We said our good byes and left. I still had to do some shopping before my lunch was over.

Once I got back to my desk, all I could think about were those black lace panties Tina was wearing. I caught a quick glimpse of them in the restroom. It wouldn't be natural if I didn't look. I looked behind me carelessly every now and then just so I could see when Tina came back from lunch. She finally walked up behind me.

"Tina, when did you start sitting over here?"

"Last Saturday. The other girl who used to sit here quit."

We continued to exchange small talk for a few minutes. We didn't want to get in trouble with the boss. It wasn't long, however, before she asked me a question about the Walmart. I was surprised to say the least.

"Tina, did you like my panties?

I didn't say anything at first. Finally I answered.

"Yes. I wouldn't wear them to work. I'd only wear them on a special night with my studband.

"Girl, that's all I wear," Tina said and smiled.

We forgot that we were at work as we talked a few more minutes and laughed about crazy stuff. She asked if I had plans for lunch the next day and if not, could we have lunch together. I consented and for the rest of the day, we worked diligently and didn't talk.

The next day, I suggested that we go to McDonald's for lunch. For some reason, I had a serious craving for some Mickey D fries and a chocolate sundae. I arrived first. I knew she would be running a few minutes late because at the last minute, the supervisor had some extra work for her to do. I went to the bathroom to wash my hands and freshen up even though I hated going to that McDonald's restroom. At lunchtime, all the construction workers pack the place. Whenever a woman walks in, they turn into vultures waiting for their next big meal.

I was about to leave when I looked up and saw her standing there. I couldn't help but wonder if she intentionally waits for me to go to the bathroom just to talk to me candidly.

"Girl, you must walk on air because you sneak up on me all the time," I said to her and headed for the door. She walked closely behind me.

She whispered in my ear, "I'm sorry."

It turned me on. She bit my neck and then held up one finger in front of me and said, "Shhhhhhh."

She squeezed my breasts with both hands and kept biting and kissing me on my neck. "Denise, let me give you want you need," she said.

I quickly moved away from her as I fixed my clothes and combed my hair back into place.

"I'm in a relationship, Tina."

She backed away from me, but she had a frown on her face. She was still very persistent.

"You should let me make love to you."

"You don't know me like that!"

I tried to open the door, but it was locked. Tina still stood against the wall. It looked like she was about to cry, but I didn't even stop to ask why. It didn't matter. I was shocked. I left out of McDonald's angry. Even worse, I left without my fries and chocolate sundae. I went back to work and sat at my desk like nothing ever happened. I had to make sure we didn't see or talk to each other for the rest of the day. Tina was definitely a beautiful woman, but I was in a relationship. That didn't stop me from being attracted to her, though. Sometimes throughout the day, I would sneak a peek at her. Since that day at McDonald's, Tina and I haven't spoken to one another.

I figured I could get caught up on my work if I went to work on Tuesday since it was my off day and grab a few overtime hours as well. The universe was not on my side. As soon as I walked into the office, Tina was there, too. I didn't expect to see her. Tuesdays were her off day, too. My forehead started to sweat so badly, I had to get a wet wipe out of my bag to wipe it.

With a sarcastic tone, I asked, "So are you working overtime, too?"

"You see me here, don't you?" She gave me a devilish smile. "Denise, are you still mad at me about what happened at McDonald's? Damn, that was almost three weeks ago."

I got up out of my seat as if I didn't even hear her talking to me. When I turned to respond to her, she wasn't even in her seat anymore. I didn't see her leave. I had to use the bathroom, but I didn't want to go in because she would probably be there. But, I couldn't hold it any longer. I walked in the bathroom and sure enough, there she was. She apologized and acted like she was the sweetest person in the world.

"Denise," she said, "you need to loosen up."

"Whatever," I said and walked out.

At that moment, I knew Tina was going to be a problem. I tried to take my breaks late on purpose, but it didn't matter. She'd be on her break, too. I wanted to say something to someone, but I didn't want to start any drama at work. One day, I went to the local barbecue place for lunch. When I went in the bathroom, I locked the door because for some reason, it became routine for Tina to always pop up everywhere I was. For the first time, I was looking at myself in the mirror, alone, thick and beautiful as ever. Still, no matter how much I tried, I couldn't get Tina off my mind. What was she doing to me? I picked up my purse and walked out the door. She did it again.

"Where do you think you're going?"

I couldn't control myself around her. She kissed me and before I knew it, she had me pinned up against the wall. I was in the corner with my pants halfway down, my breasts were hanging out of my shirt, and my arms were in the air above my head. I was moaning uncontrollably. I couldn't fight her off and I didn't want to either. I was actually enjoying it. Her hands traveled down the front of my pants. She finally reached my pussy, which was wet with excitement. She stroked me. My moans were so loud. She rubbed my pussy with one hand and grabbed my ass with the other. She gently bit my neck and then kissed me. I just let her have her way with me. I could hardly move. My moans became louder and louder. I called out her name with a faint voice. She gently bit my bottom lip and then kissed me again very seductively. I came hard. I was so weak, I almost fell to the floor, but I caught myself.

She whispered in my ear. "Stop fighting me. You know you want it."

I only had enough energy to pull my pants up, wash my hands, and freshen up again. I walked out feeling as if everybody in the restaurant heard us. Hell, I didn't care at that point. I looked forward to our little sexual escapades from then on. I definitely released some built up stress by being with Tina. I hated we couldn't get my baby involved. Tina hated studs. I told her my baby would love to watch us, but she got so mad at me.

Tina was weird sometimes. She acted as if she didn't even know me sometimes, but she still wanted to freak me in the bathroom. It was driving me crazy. I couldn't go on like this. We had a lot in common, however. I loved the way she could change her style. One day she looked like a video vixen and the next day, she looked like a mom going to a PTA meeting.

Tina rocked some bad ass wigs, too, and her shoe collection was to die for. But, I don't have time for heels every day. I only wore heels on the weekends when my studband and I went to Atlanta. I really do miss going to Atlanta. We haven't been there in a while. Tina said she'd go with me one day, but I didn't think that would be possible.

I needed to end our relationship. It was getting out of hand. Tina had so much control over me. One day she told me to wear a skirt and no panties to work. I did it even though she wasn't even at work that day. I was so mad, but it was still okay. I got a nut, anyway. I put my hand inside my skirt right at my desk and placed my pocket rocket on my clit and I had a crazy orgasm thinking about how she made me feel. I loved it. I even sucked my fingers after it was all over. Tina turned me on to that. She rested her hand on top of mine as I masturbated. Then she would slowly suck my fingers.

I wondered if Tina was actually having sex at home. I'd love to watch Tina and her girlfriend go at it. Tina described her girl to me one day. From the description, she sounded a lot like Shun. I felt bad about cheating. I didn't know what came over me, but I couldn't keep going on like this. I've found myself looking for Tina all the time and wondering if we'd hook up again and have a little fun. I wasn't looking for her today at work. I decided to go home.

When I got home, Shun was waiting at the door for me. She had been very patient with me, considering I gave her every possible excuse in the world for not having sex. I'd say I was tired or my stomach hurt. I have even acted as if my cycle lasted longer than normal. None of that worked today. When I unlocked the door, she was standing there.

"Baby, I have waited over three weeks for some of that wet-wet. I don't want to hear any more excuses." She looked me in the eye and spoke with authority. Her patience was gone as she reached for my purse and pointed upstairs. "Just give me your purse and go do whatever you need to do."

"Where are the kids?" I asked.

"Nobody is here but you and me."

She assured me that the kids were at their friends' house for a birthday party. I put her off long enough. I couldn't keep doing that. After all, she was my spouse and I shouldn't keep denying her the simple pleasures of sex.

I walked in the room and she bent me over the bed immediately. Her orange and white University of Tennessee basketball shorts were down just enough so her strap-on could hang out. Normally she would take her time and our foreplay action would be off the chain. But, she didn't have any mercy on me and she was horny as hell. The way she put it inside me, I almost dropped to my knees from the thrust alone.

Shun spoke to me in the most aggressive tone I've every heard. "'Shawty, I don't want to wait this long for what is mine. Let this be a warning."

I had my first orgasm in a week with my baby just from her talking to me like that. I loved that thug shit. Shun continued to fuck me and I wanted it bad. I was a bad girl and I needed the kind of punishment she was dishing out. I tried to talk, but I the words wouldn't come out. I loved it. Tina didn't have shit on this. Shun had me where I wanted to be, on my hands and knees for some doggy style action. Although she was a little more aggressive than normal, I loved it. It had been long enough, I suppose.

I came several times and she knew it. It turned her on. I was throwing the pussy right back at her. She started thrusting and faster, harder and harder. She was about to have an orgasm. I looked back at her. She had her hands on my ass and was pulling me back as I moved forward. Her head was raised high as she looked at the ceiling while biting her bottom lip. She had me open. She couldn't take it anymore. My wet pussy was driving her crazy. I let her have her way with me. She was squeezing my ass so tight. I looked over at the mirror so I could get a better view of her face. That's when I saw Tina.

Was I dreaming, or was that really Tina I saw hiding in the corner looking as if she wanted to hurt Shun. At that point, I didn't care. Dream or not, I gave Tina the look of death. Then I decided to make Tina mad. I let her know how good Shun was making me feel by my facial expressions. I bit my lip, closed my eyes, and screamed Shun's name. I was still distracted by the fact that Tina was in my house. How in the hell did she get in? I kept throwing the pussy at Shun harder and harder. She had no idea that Tina was in the house. Tina stood there mad as hell. She watched Shun fuck me good and give me the best orgasm ever. We finally kissed. Tina got madder. Shun and I both had an orgasm. Shun looked up at me, but I was scared as hell. I thought she saw Tina.

"Damn, baby. We need to wait a few weeks more often."

"No, baby. I don't want to wait that long again," I said as I smiled at Shun. "I'm going to the bathroom to take a shower. I'll be right back."

"Aight, Shawty," she said as she popped me on the ass when I walked by her. She laid on her back across the bed and took off her strap-on, which was still wet and shining from the hurting she put on me. I knew she was about to roll a blunt. Shun couldn't have seen Tina because once she started rolling a blunt, she had tunnel vision. She always focused her attention on having it being just the right size and nothing else. I walked out of the bedroom and down the hall to the bathroom. Tina followed softly behind me and I shut the door with force.

Shun must have thought I was crazy. I turned the shower on so Shun couldn't hear us talk. For some reason, Tina thought we were a couple.

"Bitch, you need to get out of my house. How did you even get in?"

I went crazy. Surely Shun wasn't cheating on me with Tina. We hadn't had sex in a while, but, I knew she loved me enough not to do some shit like cheat. So that wasn't an issue for me.

"I have a key," Tina said.

I was screaming so loudly, that Shun came out of the room, knocked on the door and asked if I was okay.

"I'm fine, baby," I assured her. "I was just talking on the phone." I heard her walk back down the hall.

"How in the hell do you just walk into my house?" I went on to tell Tina that either she let this be the last time we saw each other or I would have her arrested. She agreed reluctantly.

"Denise, you shouldn't do that to me. I turned away from her to get in the shower and told her to get out of my house the same way she came in. She left without incident and without Shun noticing her.

As soon as I got out of the shower, I called Mrs. Johnson, my counselor and the only African American psychologist in the downtown area. I usually saw her every day after work, but I told Shun I was working overtime. Mrs. Johnson's assistant, Sandra, answered. I needed to see Mrs. Johnson right then, but Sandra said she left already. It was an emergency, I assured Sandra. Recognizing the urgency in my voice, Sandra checked Mrs. Johnson's calendar.

"The first available appointment is tomorrow at 9:00 a.m. Can you make it then?"

"Yes!"

I was biting my fingernails and pacing the sidewalk the next day at 8:45 a.m. At 9:01, Sandra opened the door and I walked into Mrs. Johnson's office. We had been in session for about a half hour. I explained to her what happened between Tina and me. Our session was interrupted.

"Doctor Johnson," I heard Sandra say on the intercom. "You have an urgent call on line two." Mrs. Johnson insisted that we take a short break. I had to use the bathroom anyway.

Not only was Mrs. Johnson's office nicely decorated, so was the restroom. It was breathtaking. There were so many mirrors on the walls. I could see myself from all kinds of angles. I could tell it was decorated with a woman's touch. All of a sudden, Tina was standing behind me.

What the fuck! How did she know I was here? Was she following me after work and everywhere else I went? This bitch was crazy! I shouted for Mrs. Johnson and tried to run to the door, but Tina blocked the exit.

"Denise, I told you I would get what I wanted and I want you." Her tone was a lot different than she normal. She grabbed me and pushed me against the wall. "Denise, either you are going to be with me or you aren't going to be with anyone."

"Tina, please," I yelled. Mrs. Johnson is just around the corner." I tried to fight Tina off me.

"Fuck that bitch," Tina shouted. "She's trying to come between us anyway." I told her to stop, but she wouldn't. She overpowered me and had me against the wall near the sink. She ripped my shirt open. The top three buttons popped off. My bra was showing and so were my breasts. She pulled my skirt up to my waist and pulled my panties off so hard they ripped. She shoved them in my mouth and told me to shut up. I tried to make myself believe that I didn't want it, but I really did. She grabbed my breast with her left hand and her right hand massaged my pussy. I wanted to fight her, but I couldn't. I was so weak. She bit my neck as she did before. Shit, I was at my counselor's office and here I was doing this. However, I couldn't allow this to continue. I stopped fighting her and started to enjoy what she was doing to me. I felt the cum on my inner thigh.

"Denise, I knew you wanted to cum for me."

Suddenly, the restroom door flew open. It was Mrs. Johnson.

"Denise, what are you doing?"

I pushed Tina off me. "Oh my God, Mrs. Johnson. It's not me. It's Tina. See, everywhere I go she comes."

Tina and I looked at Mrs. Johnson, who was standing there as if she needed a psychologist. I pulled up my clothes with tears in my eyes. Before I could say anything, Mrs. Johnson stopped me.

"Denise, stop it! Don't look in the mirror anymore. Denise, I don't see anyone in here but you. I looked over at the sink and Tina was standing there smiling back at me with a devilish look on her face. I looked back at Mrs. Johnson.

"What are you talking about, Mrs. Johnson? Tina is right here."

"Denise, turn around. Don't look in the mirror. If Tina's behind you in the mirror, she will be there if you turn around."

I turned around and Tina wasn't there. I cried even more. Mrs. Johnson asked me to get myself together and come out of the restroom. She gave me some towels to wipe my tears.

"What's going on with me?"

"Denise," she said and then hesitated for a brief moment. "You have C.M.D., which is Compulsive Masturbation Disorder and M.P.D, Multiple Personality Disorder." She went on to tell me what the terms meant. She said they may have been triggered by my uncontrollable urges to masturbate.

"Therefore, Denise, Tina is really your alter ego. That's who you want to be. Denise you have become so weak that Tina has taken over you. You allowed Tina to create a sexual relationship with you. Now that we know what you have, you should come back tomorrow so that we can map out a plan to get both disorders under control."

I left Mrs. Johnson's office both relieved and terrified. If Tina was my alter ego, how do I get rid of her? What would Shun say? After hours of reflection, I came up with my own solution. Shun knew how to fuck me just right with a strap-on, but Tina knew just the right way to touch my pussy and make me cum hard. I could have them both. It wasn't really cheating, I suppose. I could have the best of both worlds. Maybe I could bring Tina in and have Shun at the same time. That was the plan. I cancelled my appointment with Mrs. Johnson the next day. Once I got home, I went straight to Shun.

"Let's try something different," I asked as I took off my clothes and stood in front of her.

76

An Eye for an Eye

Shunta Thomas-White

I was up early in the morning again and there was still nothing for me to do. I was so tired of being in the house that I changed the whole layout around and cleaned everything in it at least twice. I've been doing nearly everything possible just to keep myself busy. It was so quiet. I hated being home alone, but sometimes that was just how things worked out.

I almost jumped out of my skin when the phone rang. I didn't want to answer it, but I was expecting an important phone call. I was in the middle of planning a surprise birthday party for Toni on Friday. I was able to get a copy of Toni's friends and close associates' email address and phone numbers and sent them all an invitation to the party. I know she would be surprised when she saw everybody.

I answered the phone anyway, still pretending to be sleep but not really knowing for sure who it was. However, I knew there could only be one person who would call me before the roosters started to crow and that was my mother. I guess right.

"Hello, Mom," I said.

"Shunta, is that you," she asked and sounding surprised.

"Yes, Mother. Who else would be answering my phone this early in the morning?"

"Baby, you don't want me to answer that do you?"

"Ha, ha, very funny, Mother. Now look Ma, I don't feel like talking about how you feel about Toni or whether or not she is cheating on me."

"Shunta, don't you ever take that tone of voice with me," she yelled in a very firm voice.

"Sorry, Mom. I know you have my best interest in mind, but I will talk to you later, Ma."

"Okay, baby, just remember I'm always here for you if you ever need me."

"I won't forget. I love you."

"I love you, too, baby."

"Ma!" I screamed into the phone just before she hung up. "Please don't plan anything for Friday because I'm really going to need you for the party."

"I'll be there with bells on," she said and assured me that she wouldn't miss it for the world. She said it with some degree of apprehension. I knew she thought that I was crazy for sitting at home and never doing anything or going anywhere. I stopped everybody from coming over to visit and I very seldom went anywhere with my homegirls. My life pretty much resembled that of a housewife from the 1950's and here it was sixty years later and I was the millennium version of June Cleaver. But this was my choice and it was my way of showing Toni that I was really there for her whenever she needed me and no one could get in the way of that.

I put everything aside to meet Toni's every need. My homegirls thought I was crazy, but until I decided to do anything different, nothing would change. I was going to be there waiting on Dr. Toni Annette White hand and foot. Toni knew that without me, she wouldn't be where she is today. She dropped out of school in the 12th grade and I pushed her to go back to school and she did. She went on to pursue a medical degree and finally passed the state boards.

It wasn't that I didn't know Toni. Shit, I knew her better than she knew herself. I was just comfortable where I was. Although I didn't see Toni much, it was fine with me. I knew she loved me, but she just had a busy schedule. A lot of patients depended on her. At least that's what I convinced myself to believe. Lately she has been coming home feeling so tired, but thanks to her beautiful wife, she didn't have to do anything. I loved her so much.

Sometimes it was hard for me to believe that my wife was the same little girl that used to sneak out of her mother's house at age seventeen then steal her father's truck to come and eat my pussy all day. And she ate it all day, too. Just the thought about that brought back some delightful memories. Toni has come a long way because I had a few bite marks on my pussy when she first started going down on me and she didn't know the first thing about strapping although I made her feel like she did. I was told once by an older stud to never take a stud's ego away.

Man, I loved Toni so much. She was truly my whole life and I couldn't imagine life without her. I couldn't just keep sitting around thinking about the past and being bored again in the house. I decided to get out of this house today and go find something to do. Toni was booked solid today with patients so she would be leaving the office really late. Regardless of what time she arrived home, dinner would be hot and ready when she got there.

Trina Harris

I was going to play this shit as long as I could. I knew I was in love with Toni. We really started out as just friends. But I didn't know how much longer I was going to be able to hide this. I fell in love with Toni. I started saying "fuck it" whenever it came to her wife. Why should I be second to her? I was the one who had to listen to the stories about their sexual problems and other shit. I've always wanted Toni for myself, but I played the "save the relationship role." I really didn't give a shit about them fixing their relationship. I wanted Toni for myself.

I heard that Shunta asked a few people if our relationship was anything more than just friendship. Like I would ever slip up and let her know that I loved her wife and I was trying to make her mine. One day, I will tell her ass the truth so she can finally satisfy her curiosity. I even threatened Toni by saying I'd tell Shunta, but she begged me not to.

There have been times when I felt bad about our secret relationship because I've known them for a long time. I used to live a few buildings from them. That was during the time that Toni and I would simply talk on a friendship level, nothing else. Toni would be outside early in the morning as I walked my little brother to the bus stop. On most days, she sat on the tailgate of her homeboy's truck smoking a blunt wearing nothing more than a wife beater, belt, and jeans. She was so greasy from her job.

She worked 3rd shift so when she was getting off work, her wife was headed out the door to school. Toni was in school also, but her classes were late in the morning. At the time, I didn't know what type of work her wife did, but I knew Toni worked in a factory. I saw Toni every day on the back of that truck smoking a blunt.

Toni and Shunta always appeared to be happy and I envied that. I had a crush on Toni a long time ago. We've been seeing each other on the low for about two months now. Since we've been seeing each other, I guess Toni felt guilty because she moved Shunta into a nice little house about three or four miles away from the apartment we were staying in and she moved me, too. She made it possible for me to move also, but it was really on a friend level. I paid Toni in blunts. After that I didn't see her for a while. I gave my new number to a mutual friend and she said she would get it to Toni.

I didn't know that Toni and I would be where we were today. At first, I thought I just wanted to chill and smoke like we used to do. Toni was a doctor. However, she had no problem coming to the hood to smoke some of that sticky icky with me. I'd see Toni and Shunta in the club from time to time. Toni and I talked in the club. But, Shunta would always come over to kiss and hug Toni right there in front of me. All along I wondered if this bitch knew I'd be the one fucking her girl in the end. Toni talked to a lot of women in the club so I guess Shunta never thought anything about us talking. Shunta would say hello and then she'd make her rounds around the club for networking. She was really popular around the lesbian community.

I didn't know what Shunta said to Toni, but one night Toni came over my house. She said she had some shit on her mind and needed to smoke. We smoked about five blunts and then we fucked all night long with no limits. Shit, I did everything to her and she did everything to me. Shit, it's been two months and Shunta still didn't have a clue. I haven't seen Shunta in a while because I don't go to the gay clubs a lot. Honestly, I didn't care if I never saw her as long as Toni was fucking me. That was all I wanted, at least in the beginning.

Lately, I've wanted Toni full time and I was determined to get exactly what I wanted. I heard through the grapevine that Shunta was planning Toni a surprise party. If I told Toni that I was coming, she would curse me the fuck out. But, I wouldn't miss that party if my life dependent on it. I wanted to see Toni's face when everybody surprised her.

Toni and I actually have a lot in common. Toni liked to watch bitches with big asses walk by. She enjoyed fishing, playing X-Box, and smoking, which was right up my alley. I made up my mind that I would always be there for Toni whenever she just wanted to chill. My door would always be open. We have had some good times together. That was at least until I was time for her to go home to the wife.

While Shunta was sitting at home cooking and cleaning I was smoking a few blunts and riding the hell out of Toni's strap-on. I wanted to get as much of that strap-on as I could get. I've told Toni before that I didn't really care for fucking with the same strap-on she fucked her wife with. But she'd just pull out that gold wrapper Magnum XL and I couldn't say no. When I saw her strap-on, no matter how many times I've seen it, my pussy took over my body. Before I knew it, I was bent over the couch and Toni's strap-on was in my pussy so deep, I couldn't even move.

We really started out as friends. It was Toni's idea to continue. I've tried to act like I wanted to end it. I felt bad at first. I really respected her wife. She was successful, pretty and she dressed nicely. But from what Toni said in the past, everything wasn't what it appeared to be.

Toni White

The lab finally brought Mrs. Williams's lab results after I had to call and request them several times.

"Knock, knock, Mrs. Williams. Your test results are here and everything looks good. All the tests were negative and that's wonderful news."

"Oh my God, Dr. White. Thanks."

"Don't thank me, thank the Lord."

"I was so worried about this test. I've been cheating on my spouse and I didn't want to give her anything. I just wanted to be sure."

"Well, Mrs. Williams, you have some celebrating to do. Be careful out there and I will see you in a year. Do you have any questions?"

"No, ma'am."

"Well you have a good day."

Finally, I was able to sit down in my office for a minute. That Mrs. Williams was just too much. She worried about any little thing because she always cheated on her spouse. She was what I called "tri-sexual." She would try anyone sexually and do just about anything. As her physician, I had to listen, just in case she mentioned anything I should be concerned about. She panicked over the smallest things. I looked at my watch only to realize I was running late for my next appointment.

Damn, sometimes I felt older than I really was. I didn't know why I was complaining. I was a successful physician. I had everything I could ever want. I graduated from Howard University. I was an honorary member of the Alpha Phi. I had a six bedroom home in Atlanta's most prestigious neighborhood. The only thing that was missing was a child and my wife and I were working on that. I had the best wife anyone could ask for. She was a real good woman and I loved her very, very much. Hands down, she was the best thing to ever happen to me. We've been together so long, she could finish my sentences. However, no matter how good she was to me, I just wasn't in love with her anymore.

I planned on telling her, but I just couldn't bring myself to do it. I knew Shunta would stand by me no matter what, but my secret would hurt her. I've been seeing a therapist for the last six months because lately, things have gotten out of hand.

"Knock, knock Dr. White. You have one more patient.

"Okay," I said as I gathered my notes and took one last look at Shunta's picture on my desk.

Janea Carter

Man, what took Dr. White so long? I was lying there on the table staring at the ceiling and shivering like crazy. Shit, I should have brought a blanket with me. It was so cold in the exam room. I had no choice but to lay on my back naked with my feet in the stirrups and freeze halfway to death with a thin little piece of sheet to comfort me.

I was glad that I made the appointment late in the day. I had waited for a long time. I couldn't believe a year already had passed so soon. Where did the time go? Each year my sister and I faithfully had our pap smear and mammogram test done. Since my family had a long history of breast and cervical cancer, I made certain that I didn't miss any appointment. Therefore, if something ever came up, it could be detected early enough to fight it. I don't know what doctor my sister had inspecting her goods, but there was only one doctor for me and that was Dr. White.

Dr. White was an excellent physician and I felt very comfortable whenever I talked to her. Her office was filled with awards, recommendations, and countless certifications and degrees. Dr. White had an all lesbian staff. How she managed that I didn't know. It was a plus for me. I was a lesbian, too. I waited very patiently because I knew Dr. White had a huge patient list.

Usually I only had to wait in the office for about an hour or so, but today, it took a while longer. I was okay, though. I brought this book with me called Love and Liberation written by Sharon Smith. I only read a few pages, but it seemed like a real page turner. I was happy to have something to keep my mind occupied rather than going to sleep even though it was so peaceful in the office.

The only thing I heard was that pretty, young, big breasted office manager, Katrina, calling Dr. White over the intercom. She had the sexiest voice I've ever heard. I wondered if she would be at Dr. White's surprise birthday party on Friday. I wouldn't miss it for the world. I already had my dress I prayed that my Jimmy Choo purse would arrive by then.

"Knock, knock." I damn near fell off the table when I heard the knock at the door.

"Come in."

"Hi, Mrs. Carter. My name is Keba McRay. I just wanted to let you know that Dr. White is still with a patient and she'll be with you in about 15 minutes."

There was something about that Keba. She looked very sneaky, especially with all those hickeys on her neck and the visible scratch marks on her arms. I just shook my head and thought how unprofessional she looked. Then again, there could have been something else going on with her.

"Okay, thanks, Keba," I said. I knew that 15 minutes really meant about 30 minutes, but I didn't complain. It was cool.

"Keba, could you call me Janea, instead?" She consented.

Shunta Thomas-White

I really enjoyed myself today. It was so refreshing to go to The Uptown Spa and be pampered from head to toe. I got everything done for tonight's dinner and the surprise party. Toni's AMEX Black Card came in handy for the things I needed to get. Toni should be home in an hour or two and I was way overdue for some of her good loving. I had a very special night planned for us.

We hadn't had sex in two months. My vibrator had been used so much, it wouldn't move even with fresh batteries. The plan tonight was to get some serious action in the sheets.

I was going to cook Toni's favorite dinner- steak and potatoes, a salad with cucumbers and

Italian dressing along with my famous homemade sweet tea. I'd only wear my stylish red kitchen apron and a pair of Baker's shoes. I was saving my Jimmy Choo's to wear at the party. I prayed my purse was here by then, too. I ordered it two weeks ago. I also planned to have the room filled with candles and a little smooth R&B music in the background. And for dessert, she'd enjoy a delicious helping of sweet strawberries and whip cream-on me. I couldn't wait. I had some serious love that needed to be set free and only she could do it.

Trina Harris

Toni said she would be over after work. She told Shunta she was working late. We were going to grab a quick dinner and then head to the park for a walk. From there, it was off to my apartment. We'd probably roll a few blunts and smoke while we walked. All she had to do was change clothes. She said she'd start an argument with Shunta so she could have an excuse for staying out longer. I didn't give a fuck what she did as long as she was with me tonight. I told all my peeps not to come by or call me and they better not. No one should knock on my door, not even my ex. She came over from time to time just to talk about shit, but even she knew not to come over without calling first. Shunta might be tripping tonight. I only wanted to chill with Toni tonight because I knew I wouldn't be able to get any lovin' tomorrow. She said she had to work all day and Friday was the surprise birthday party.

Toni liked that sexy feminine shit so I came out of my normal routine. I hoped she'd like it because I really wanted to put on a pair of shorts and a big T-shirt. But, I decided to try that girly shit.

Shunta had Toni on lockdown, at least that's what Toni told me. Who knew? If Toni lied to her she has probably lied to me, too. At any rate, I was ready for tonight. I had my hair pulled back in a ponytail because the last time I left it down, Toni left my hair so fucked. But, I didn't complain one bit. I was her home girl. That was what we wanted everybody to think. It didn't matter how I looked as long as I was that feminine freak she liked when she was in this pussy. After tonight I wouldn't see Toni until after the party so I had to make sure we engaged in some of the freakiest ass slapping and bitch calling sex we ever had.

With the night I've planned, there was no way she would have enough energy to fuck Shunta's pretty ass. She told me that she really wanted to make her only woman and that she wanted to visit a few pawn shops to look for a ring. For some reason, going to the mall was out of the question.

Toni White

I finally left the office. I was ready to get some pussy. My birthday was tomorrow. I couldn't wait to see what

89

Shunta got me this year. Each year she outdid herself. I knew it would be something nice. I knew I wasn't the wife I should have been, either but Shunta never complained. I loved my wife, but I had a problem that kept me from being faithful to her. I was working hard to solve that problem, at least that's what I tried to convince myself. I couldn't worry about it even though I was paying top dollar for a therapist. I was about to go to Trina's house to get some of that wild ass sex.

She called me and said she was waiting on me to come and tap that ass before I went home to Shunta. Trina was like a homegirl that I could fuck any way I like. I could talk to her about the game, while smoking a blunt and looking at some big ass walking by and she didn't trip on me. Trina wasn't attractive to me in a femme way unless she was naked. That's what I wanted anyway. Whenever she got taste of ecstasy, she'd let me do anything to her. It wasn't that Shunta wouldn't do the same, but for some reason, I felt bad doing my wife like that. It was just different coming from someone else.

I've looked at pussy all day. One would think I wouldn't want to see another one for weeks. But, I'm addicted to pussy. I just love pussy and all its different shapes, sizes, tastes, and smells. Having, Mrs. Carter as my last patient really got me horny. Her pussy was so pretty. It was shaved just like my wife's. I looked at it and almost forgot what I was supposed to be doing as her doctor. I wanted to just kiss it. Instead, I finished the exam and got ready to go home. I kept trying to forget about her, but all I could think about was sliding my two fingers in her pussy to check her cervix. That really turned me on. She was lying there so beautiful and she smelled so good. She was wearing Juicy Couture, a perfume I've bought a few times for my wife.

I hated the fact that I lusted for my patients, but I couldn't help it. It was part of my addiction. Dr. Johnson, a therapist I've been seeing for the past six months, hadn't put a name on my strange addiction yet, but she stated she would look into it for me. Mrs. Carter was one of my faithful patients who had been coming to me for at least five years. I knew her wife, Jo, a maintenance manager at Dr. Johnson's office. I was glad Jo thought that Dr. Johnson and I were just talking business. If anyone knew that I was actually Dr. Johnson's patient and that I was trying to deal with my pussy addiction, I would lose my job and possibly my license. God only knew what would happen with me and Shunta.

I had to get myself together. I didn't know how I was going to see Trina tonight and chill with my wife. I was determined to do it, though. Since I was so fucking hungry and horny, I did something I never usually do. I called Shunta and asked if she wanted to have dinner with me no matter what time I got there. She eagerly said yes. She asked me to come straight home when I was finished working so we could have dinner at home. I consented. I loved Shunta because I always got what I wanted from her and more. I wanted to make love to her tonight. The sad part about it was that I was going to imagine she was Mrs. Carter and we are going to role play.

I still wanted to get some of that wild and crazy sex from Trina before going home. I told her to be ready and we would go to the Riverwalk. That was the place I really wanted to fuck her anyway. Shit, I hated going to her apartment because the neighbors are so fucking nosy and I didn't need my business out in the streets. I was going to bend that nice ass over the rail, grab her by the back of her neck, and shove this strap-on so far inside her, she should couldn't help but scream. Knowing that freaky ass bitch, she would enjoy every bit of it.

I didn't want to drive the Lamborghini over to the hood because it attracted too much attention. I went to the parking deck by my office and picked up my old truck. It would probably cause a lot of attention, too. It was egg yolk yellow, but I loved that truck. My dad gave it to me years ago.

Janea Carter

Kimberly, the chic from the Jimmy Choo store, called to tell me the bag I had been waiting for finally arrived. I told her I would be there today to pick it up.

"That's cool, Mrs. Carter," she replied. "There's only two and you and another lady already have them reserved. The good thing is you both have different colors."

"Great, I'm on my way."

I picked up my bag from the Jimmy Choo store and finally made it home after a long day. Jo, who I've called my spouse for six years now, wasn't home yet. I decided to call her before taking a shower. For some reason, when I left Dr. White's office, I was so wet.

She didn't answer the phone. I could have been looking into things a little too much, but everybody knew that if a person's cell phone rang four times, that person was looking at the damn caller id. If the phone was turned off, it rang once and went to voicemail. I got the damn voicemail after the fourth ring. I wanted to laugh because I heard Jo's voice on the voicemail trying to sound all hard and shit. "What's up? You called the right person, but at the wrong time so leave "ya boi" a message one." I just hung up the phone. I was thinking "yeah right." "Ya boi?" If people only knew that I was really the "boi" in this relationship. I was a femme in the streets stud in the sheets, but I kept that a secret. I wondered what she was doing. She always answered her phone.

Jo is the maintenance manager for this counselor, Mrs. Johnson. She was pretty good from what I heard. My friend, Denise, went to her about some bitch name Tina that wouldn't leave her alone. I wished Denise would have let me get at that bitch. For some reason, Tina never showed up when Denise and I would schedule a meeting with her. I would have ripped her a new one.

I wondered how much work Jo had to do at an office building that small. I was so tired, though, that I really didn't care. My plan was to take a shower, watch a little TV, and then take a nap. Damn, I felt so horny and drained after leaving Dr. White's office. I didn't know what she

93

did during my session, but I had no energy at all. I walked upstairs and got a fresh pair of panties out my drawer. I absolutely killed Victoria's Secrets last week. I bought nearly every damn pair of panties in the store, according to Jo. My mother always told me that a woman could never have enough underwear.

I closed the drawer and as I walked in the bathroom, I tripped and almost broke my neck on Jo's damn Timberland boots on the floor. She always left our room fucked up. But if I went into that playroom of hers, she would die. I guess that would be understandable. She put so much work into that room. But the next time I saw a boot in the middle of the floor, her ass was going to sleep in the playroom. She'd like that anyway.

Jo's playroom was every gamer's dream. The color scheme, which I called the Scarface colors, was red, black, and white. The walls were covered with Scarface posters. There was a couch, recliner, and two game chairs. A 52 inch black Plasma HD TV hung on the wall and was connected to a Playstation 3 and an Xbox 360. On the right side of the TV were two stands, one for games and the other had all the movies that a true gangster would love. I loved the room, but whenever she was in there playing a game, she had the speakers up so loud, they hurt my ears. The game I loved to watch her play was Hitman. Sometimes when I wanted a good laugh, I would go to the door and just watch her play. Oh my God, it was the funniest thing in the world to see. She acted like she was really a part of the action.

She'd talk to the TV, make crazy gestures, and everything. But, that was my baby.

Shunta Thomas-White

Toni looked like she couldn't breathe while she ate my pussy. Shit, I didn't care. She hadn't eaten my pussy for a few weeks. This was my way for punishing her.

"Oh yes, baby. Right there!" I continued to hold her head deep down in my pussy. I was so weak from the first two orgasms, I could barely talk. I grabbed the back of Toni's hair. Just when I thought she really couldn't breathe, I lifted her head up just enough so she could catch her breath and then shoved her head back in my pussy.

"Eat me, dammit! I want it. Yes, right there! Lick it, suck my clit. Oh my God, Toni. Yes, I love it."

I couldn't help but scream her name. I continued to hold her head down on my pussy. She was finally giving me what I wanted.

"Toni, I'm about to cum, baby," I yelled. I squeezed her head tighter.

I had been holding this in for two weeks. I knew I wasn't going to be good for anything but sleep after this. I couldn't hold my orgasm anymore my legs were so numb my toes were curled up so tight, I couldn't even straighten them out. I heard the phone ring, but I didn't want to stop Toni from eating my pussy. I just let it ring, but the ringing seemed to be getting louder and louder. Finally, I reached over to get the phone while Toni was eating my pussy. It was Kimberly from the Jimmy Choo store.

"Mrs. Thomas –White? This is Kimberly. Your purse has arrived."

I opened my eyes and I noticed there was no one in the room with me. Talk about a wet dream. The phone was really ringing, but I was dreaming all that time. Toni was still not home. I waited for her for two mother fucking hours last night. She didn't call. I was so worried. I wanted to call the police because she should have been home. I decided to go by Toni's office and see if she was at work. I didn't know what was happening to us, but I felt I was not enough for her.

Crying, I called my mother. I didn't want to because I knew she would start preaching and saying "I told you so." She still promised to be at the party to help me out. I didn't want to mention that didn't come home. Somehow, she knew it anyway.

"Toni's not home yet, huh?"

"I know I'm not crazy, Ma. I know what's up. Everybody knows the doctor's office is closed by 6:00 PM. I even drove by there plenty of times at 5:30pm and she was already gone." I went on to tell her how Toni always gave me the line about working late and that she had a full day of patients. "Ma, I know Toni thinks all I'd do is sit at home and wait for her. But, I'm going to get to the bottom of this as soon as I see her."

My mother sighed at me in disbelief. "Yeah, right, Shunta. You've said that so many times before.

"I should have known something was going on anyway when I went by there a few days ago and she wasn't there. She must think I'm stupid." My voice became louder and louder as I spoke to my mother on the phone. She could tell I was really pissed off, but she just remained quiet to let me vent. I knew Toni was doing things outside the house that she didn't do with me. People sometimes get too happy when they cheat and they eventually get sloppy. They say things they don't normally say and do thing they don't normally do.

My mother and I exchanged a few more comments and eventually hung up. I knew she was mad as hell. I used to think she wanted to kill Toni, especially when she found out about Toni's will. I would be set for the rest of my life. I would never want to do anything to hurt Toni, but my mother was a different story. I really thought Toni loved me. I was just so comfortable and didn't want to leave my wife. We had a beautiful thing together, for a while at least. Shit, it's been two weeks and I haven't really seen her excerpt for a few mornings in passing when she was on her way to work.

Trina Harris

I felt so good when I got out of the shower. I knew Toni would be here within minutes. I had everything ready. I already smoked a blunt of Kush. I hoped she would be all smiles tonight when she left. I didn't plan on her leaving if everything worked out. I planned to freak Toni out. My apartment was small, but I was going to make sure I fucked Toni all over it. Suddenly, I heard a knock at the door. I knew it wasn't Toni because she knew all she had to do was get the key from under the rug on the porch. I opened the window in my room and looked down to see who could have been knocking. I didn't see anyone. I closed the window and finished drying off. I was about to put some lotion on my body when Toni came sneaking up behind me.

I turned around quickly. "Are you trying to scare me?"

She was still in her uniform and I could tell she was wearing her strap-on, too. It looked like it was about to come out of her pants.

"What's up, nigga," I said to her. "Why are you trying to scare the shit out me?" I walked closer to her without my towel, still slightly wet. "I still have four blunts left."

"Okay. I only need two and some of that ass. I have to go home tonight, Trina."

If she only knew what my plan was. She wasn't going anywhere tonight but right here in this pussy. I walked away from Toni to put on something to just walk around the house in, but Toni stopped me.

"Don't put on anything!"

I turned around and looked at her. She was lighting a blunt. I was a little chilly since I just got out of the shower. The towel was still wrapped around me. All I had on was a pair of house shoes. We watched the food channel until we finally smoked the last blunt. Then Toni just pulled me toward her and started squeezing my breasts.

"Shunta, Shunta, Shunta," she said.

I looked at her strangely and I was mad as hell. "Mother fucker, you know I'm not Shunta." She just looked up at me. I was high as hell. She looked at me like she didn't know me.

"Bitch, I know you ain't Shunta," she said with a weird and scary look on her face. "You will never be Shunta," she continued. "There is nothing you can do to ever take Shunta's place. I just wanted you to know that."

I looked at Toni and wondered where the hell all that came from. Toni was still holding me. Then she turned me around and damn near pushed me over. Normally I didn't like it when Toni fucked fuck me doggy style, but this time was different. I felt like she really didn't see me as anything but a piece of ass. She would always talk about how unhappy she was at home, but she would never say what was wrong. I knew in my heart it was just Toni's excuse to not feel guilty about what she was doing to Shunta. She'd blame it on Shunta. I knew Shunta was perfect for Toni. She could have any woman she wanted, but she had been faithful to Toni's cheating ass for years. Toni was fucking me and God knows who else for the same amount of years.

I fucked the shit out of Trina Tuesday night and last night, but I was mad as hell at her because I told that bitch I had to go home to my wife. Trina allowed me to do whatever I wanted to her and I loved it. But that's not a reason to treat Shunta like that. I'm sure she was worried all night. I knew Shunta would give me all of her in any kind of way, but I just felt funny fucking her like she was a piece of trash. Trina was an alternative. She always gave me wild, crazy, off the chain, hair grabbing, ass slapping, bitch calling, and hands around the neck type of sex. But that wasn't even enough for me. That's why I knew I could never miss my appointment with Dr. Johnson because this was getting so out of control.

I was neglecting Shunta and I never wanted that to happen. She seemed to be so happy, but I could tell she wasn't. The more I had sex with other women, the more I neglected Shunta. I was going to go home to take care of her no matter how tired I was. I needed to make a stop by my old hood before I went home. My homeboy called and said he had my package. I waited for that call for a while. I knew I would pay top dollar for it, but I needed it.

No matter how hard I tried, I couldn't stop. I was so in love with women. I could get any woman I wanted, whether they were willing to be with me or not. I've had all types of women. When they came into my office, I had a one-on-one conversation with their pussy in my mind. The best part about it is they didn't have any control of their pussy once it was in my face. Some were willing and some didn't have a clue. Shit, I tried it on Trina first and she had no idea. One night I went over there and told her that we would be role playing and she would be my patient. With Trina, it was easier than anyone else because she thought I was just giving her some water through a needle. With the other patients, I had to find other ways to give it to them. Normally I gave it to my last patient of the day. I gave it to Mrs. Carter the other day. Her pussy was everything I imagined.

I loved the ones that put up a fight. They got to meet the real Toni. It was mainly women I met in these hood clubs. But the one that really loved to fuck me and didn't care what I gave her was my nurse assistance, Keba. She loved all that wild scratching, biting, and stabbing kind of fucking. Keba was way passed what me and Trina liked to do.

With Keba, we acted things out at her house like they were really happening. I came over one day with my strap-on on. She even let me break in her house for real. I came in through the window wearing a paint ball mask. She fought with me like I was a real burglar. She was screaming and crying. Before I knew it, I hit her and put a sock in her mouth. I took that pussy like it was mine for the taking. With Keba I had to really work out. I had to eat breakfast, lunch, and dinner to keep my energy high. She always gave me a serious work out in the bedroom. One time we were role playing and we really got hurt. I had to give Keba stitches and we still had to be at work the next morning.

Janea Carter

I took my shower and was putting on panties and baby lotion. Although I had a big beautiful king size Paul Bunyon bed that I had to use steps to get in, I was going to lie on my Ashley's couch with just my panties on. I planned to let The Lifetime Movie Network watch me today even though one of my favorite movies was coming on, *The Fantasia Barrino Story*. I loved it, but it would be watching me as I slept. For some reason, I couldn't sleep so I did the only thing that worked every time.

I put my index and middle fingers in my mouth and wet them really good. Not that I needed to because I was always wet. I grabbed a sheet out of closet and placed it on the couch. I opened my legs and started rubbing my pussy with one hand and grabbed my breasts, squeezing my nipples often with the other hand. I was shaking uncontrollably. It felt so good. I was enjoying myself. I was ready to release all the stress from the day. I moaned loudly. It was almost time. Then I heard Jo sticking the key in the door. Damn. Mad as hell, I stopped and just pretended that I was asleep. She walked in and then just went straight upstairs.

Instead of this mother fucker stopping to wake me up or say hello, she took her ass upstairs and got in the shower. I opened my eyes just before she reached the top step and noticed she carried a big bag like she just came from a trip somewhere. Any normal person would be pissed if their spouse came in the house and didn't acknowledge them by saying anything. Something wasn't right.

She went in the room and I heard the shower come on. Usually when she got off work, she walked around for a while to get a beer out of the refrigerator then went in that damn playroom, but she jumped in the damn shower. Now that could only mean one of two things. Either she just had sex with someone else or she got really dirty at work today. Now I doubt she got that dirty at work. I wasn't going to let that shit worry me. As soon as I heard the shower door close, I put my fingers back in my mouth. I could still taste my pussy from earlier. My body betrayed me. I bit my lip. I rubbed my pussy with just enough pressure to keep my orgasm on the edge. I came before I knew it. I was so loud that I just knew Jo heard me. Oh well, she should've been down here satisfying me.

Damn, I did a damn good job. When I woke up, the credits from movie was rolling. The clock on the TV said 8 o'clock. I got up and went to the kitchen to get something to drink and I noticed the mail on the table. I was about to walk right by it, but I noticed the bank statement. I opened it and lost my mind at the balance. I went upstairs to see what Jo was doing and to curse her ass out.

As I approached the stairs, I heard what sounded like crying. I walked in our room and Jo was lying on the bed with a sheet over her. The bag she had with her earlier was opened and I saw some money on the bed and more of it in the bag. Jo seemed to be upset.

"Baby, what's wrong?"

"Take this money," she said and then hesitated before she spoke again. "Open a new account. I will explain the rest after the party Friday. There's more than enough in there to replace what's missing from the account."

She insisted that I go shopping for new clothes. "Go and get us something really, really nice to wear."

I didn't know what was going on. Jo was being very secretive with me. I just wanted to know where all the money went. But something was really bothering her. I got in the bed with Jo and she gave me the best oral sex I have ever had in my life. After I had what seemed like ten orgasms, we laid in each other's arms the rest of the night.

Shunta Thomas- White

Toni finally made it home early Friday morning. I was so fucking mad I didn't say anything to her. I acted like I was so happy to see her. I was, but I was still upset. I wasn't going to let anything stop me from getting some good lovin' before the party tonight. Shit, I deserved at least a 20 minute session. It would help me with that dream I had yesterday morning.

"Damn, could I be the patient right now? I knew you weren't at work. Could you make a house call for me?

She came in and sat on the couch next to me like she had been working all night. She smelled like that cheap ass Impression of Princess by Vera Wang. I had the real one. I wondered which one of her patients wore that shit.

Toni still had on her doctor's jacket. That shit turned me on so bad. Shit, I almost forgot I was mad at her ass when I noticed the strap-on. I knew she always wore it, even at work. The thought had me so wet. I told Toni to go and shower and I would warm her plate up from dinner last night or I would make her breakfast. She said she took a shower already. I just said okay.

"Happy birthday, baby," I said and gave her a hug.

She was sitting there with her long hair pulled back into a pony tail. She had very pretty hair. She said her father was from the West Indies so I guess that was where she got it from.

Toni took her jacket off. Her muscular arms were showing through her Armani shirt and was making me horny as hell. Damn, when she took the shirt and tie off, her arms looked like she was just oiled down before she got home. She slouched back on the couch, her wife beater and sports bra still on. She kept on the Armani belt and pants and that damn strap-on was bulging out of her pants as if she really had a hard on.

She wanted dinner from last night. I brought her plate to her and she just shook her head.

"Damn, now that's what's up," she said. She saw her favorite foods and smiled. "I don't know what to do with you, Shunta."

I could name a few things she could do right then. How about fuck me sometimes. I kept thinking that if I got any wetter, we'd have a flood in the house. But, I didn't say anything. I just picked up her clothes and took them upstairs while she ate.

Toni's party was tonight. I didn't want to start a fight today, but I wanted to ask her some questions. Questions like how in the hell was she fresh out of the shower at 7:00 AM? Why didn't you come home last night? Why the fuck do your arms look like you just got oiled up for a body building competition? I decided to save those questions for Saturday.

As I hung up Toni's jacket, a bag fell out of it. I opened it. There were two bottles of Haldol, which was short for Haloperidol. I took a pharmacology class and I knew that in large amounts, Haldol could be very harmful to the person taking it. The side effects were extreme drowsiness, little or no control of the muscles in the eye, tongue, jaw, or neck. I wondered why in the hell would Toni need it at her office. I needed to get to the bottom of this. I was confused. I yelled downstairs to ask Toni to come upstairs once she was done eating. She said okay, but I knew she wouldn't come.

I called my mother immediately. I didn't tell my friends my business any more. I learned that a long time ago because once they get mad, they tell everything. My mother answered the phone like she was out partying.

"Ma, what's all that noise?"

She said she was up early because she couldn't sleep. She claimed to be working on Toni's birthday surprise for the party.

"Ma, I need to talk to you. I know Toni is doing something she has no business doing. She brought home some kind of medicine that I know she didn't even need at her office." My mother just sat there listening to me. She didn't say a word, but I could tell she was just waiting for the chance to jump right in. "Ma, I know Toni has been cheating on me, too." Tears filled my eyes as I spoke.

I went on to tell her how I was tired of the lies. I didn't want to mess up her birthday, but I was simply tired. I just couldn't take it anymore. To my surprise, my mother was cool.

"Baby, don't worry about it," my mother said. She shocked the shit out of me. "Let's get through the party and then we will deal with it. You don't worry your pretty little head off. Your mother's here for you."

I dried my face off. I couldn't believe she was answering me so calmly. I knew she didn't like Toni and this would be the perfect chance for her to tell me to leave Toni. But, my mother was on the phone like "oh well, life goes on." I didn't think she took me serious.

"Toni will see," I said. "I will get the last laugh."

My mother was silent on the phone. I thought for a moment I heard her crying, but maybe I was mistaken. She never liked Toni, but she was the one who was telling me not to worry about it. I thought she was happy to hear me say I was tired and fed up. After all, she told me from the beginning that she thought Toni was cheating on me. No matter how many times someone tells you, you just have to see for yourself. Sometimes people know, but they are just too comfortable to face the situation so they deal with it until enough is enough.

Before I got off the phone with my mother, she had one more thing to put in my ear.

"Baby, when you are really, really tired of anything, you will not have to talk to anyone about it. You won't be concerned about the person's feelings or how your living arrangements will work out or if you're going to get anything out of it in the end. You will just let it all go and move on."

I knew exactly what she was talking about and I agreed. I was just mad, but not to the point where I would want to leave Toni. I just wanted her to know that I knew what she was doing.

Trina Harris

Toni came over and fucked the shit out of me last night. I started to hate her. I wanted to be more than her fucking sideline hoe. I loved our sex. If someone walked up on us fucking, they would probably think we were fighting and try to rescue one of us. Our sex was so deep, that I often got confused. I didn't know if we were out for an orgasm or trying to kill each other. But last night, Toni went too far with me. I couldn't believe she talked to me like that. Tonight was the night of the party. I couldn't wait. I was going to get that nigga for how she treated me yesterday.

I called my homeboy to see if he could find some dirt on Dr. Toni. He told me that he had been seeing Toni a lot in their hood.

"For what," I asked.

"Toni has been buying a drug called Haldol off the street. She pays a pretty penny for it, too."

"What does that shit do?"

"I'd love to try some new shit, but that shit's not for getting high. It's a downer. With the amount of shit's she's been buying, she could really kill somebody."

I wondered why in the hell she would want that. I told him I found a bottle of that shit, too when it fell out of her jacket pocket, but it was empty and there wasn't a label on it. I asked him to explain to me what the drug did and he went in great details about the side effects. After that, I was so fucking mad at Toni because I remembered one night she came over to my house. After she gave me something to drink, we were role playing and for some reason, I felt crazy. I asked her to chill with me for a few minutes to see if I was just too high or what. The next morning when I woke up, I felt like I had wet my bed. I was so drained.

The next day, I called her and she said she really enjoyed being with me the night before. I asked her what happened. All she could say was that she had a wonderful time with me. That was the first time I woke up and Toni left $100.00 on the night stand. I didn't remember anything from that night. I just knew that when I was about to get up, I felt like my legs were jello. She must have used that shit on me. It was on! I had something for her ass.

I bought a nice little black dress from Trends City. It was only $22.00. I borrowed the shoes and accessories from my homegirl because I wasn't going to buy all that shit for one night. I was going to that party. Toni had no idea there was a party and she still didn't know I was coming. I went to the neighborhood hairdresser and let her hook me up with something I called "ghetto classy."

I knew the place would be filled with those stuck up ass women that thought they were all that. My ex-girlfriend's sister was coming to pick me up and I would find a way back home. Dr. Toni had something coming to her tonight. I would have the last laugh.

Toni White

Man, this was the life. I finally made it home around 6:30 or 7:00 this morning. Shunta was beautiful as ever and again I questioned myself on why I continued to hurt her. She was truly everything a woman could want. I thought she

110

would be cursing and screaming by now because I didn't come home, but she just made sure I was happy and comfortable. I prayed that she couldn't smell this cheap ass version of Impression that was buried in my clothes. It smelled like the one Shunta had.

She was so happy to see me. She walked like the perfect wife that she was, jumping at my every request as usual. I didn't want to hurt her feelings and tell her I didn't want the dinner she made me last night, so I ate it. I knew she had something nice planned for me tonight because she asked me to eat and come upstairs and rest for a while. She said she had a nice night planned for her birthday boy.

I prayed Shunta didn't look in my pockets because I forgot I had the two bottles of medicine still in the pocket. I would have some serious explaining to do if she saw what was in there. Shunta was in nursing school and I knew she would know what the medicine is and what it was used for. She had to have felt something was in the pocket, but she just looked back and asked me to come up once I finished eating.

I was so tired. All I needed was a good meal and I would be going to sleep. Besides, I didn't want any pussy the way Trina and I fucked last night. When I got there Trina was already high. She said she smoked a blunt already and still had four more for us to share. She said she didn't want me to go home. Before I knew it, I cursed that bitch out. I thought I let that her think she had control over me because she was trying to check me. She kept asking when I was going to get the ring I promised her and that she was tired of being second to Shunta. She even told me I needed to call me wife and make up a lie and say something to allow me to be with her all night.

I couldn't believe I had plans to buy this dumb ass trick a ring or as I called it, a "keep your mother fucking mouth closed about what we do, bitch" ring. But this bitch had lost her mind and she must have forgotten what her mother fucking purpose was. So I had to remind her. I cursed her ass out calm as hell.

In no uncertain terms, I said, "bitch, first of all you serve two purposes. First, you are going to give me that pussy when I want it and how I want it. Second, when I need to talk, no matter how tired of hearing what I have to say, your mother fucking ears better be to the ground listening to everything I say when I need to vent."

I told her to never think that she was superior over my damn wife. Shunta was my life. Without her, I wouldn't know what to do. I went on to tell her that regardless of the shit I said to her while we were fucking, I wasn't going to leave my wife.

Trina thought I was going to leave Shunta and that was partly my fault. But, there was no way in the hell I would leave my wife for her ass. She was only pussy and an ear for me and I was going to buy her a ring just so she could think it was something with us. I was a physician and I couldn't risk her ghetto ass getting out of hand and fucking up what I knew without Shunta, wouldn't be possible. Bitches like Trina were trifling as hell so the ring was a "keep quiet" gift.   Plus Shunta and I were working on having a child which meant the world to me. Trina's ass didn't even have custody of her kids. From what I heard, she used to be on powder real bad and some of her family members took the kids from her. She saw her kids sometimes, but I didn't need a sometimes mother for my child.

Trina had two boys of her own and one little boy from her previous relationship with her ex-girlfriend. Trina broke her neck trying to do any and everything for that little boy, but she didn't do shit for her biological children. But, when I was in the pussy, I didn't care which child she took care of, but I knew it would never be a child of mine.

Trina was just irresponsible. She still had to ask her mother for help with her bills. Now Shunta, on the other hand, if I stopped working today, my baby would sell anything anywhere to get what we needed. There wasn't a limit on what she would do to make the house run smoothly. I knew she could do it because she has done it before. Hell, I didn't work for the first two years we were together and Shunta held the mother fucking apartment we were in down. She paid all the bills, bought food, and kept a nigga with some fresh Fila on my feet. I never worried about anything with her.

That's why I was going to make sure I was in Dr. Johnson's office on Monday because I loved my wife and I didn't want to leave her. But, if I couldn't stop this addiction of mine, I was going to leave her, my job, and all my patients. Maybe I would go overseas and be a doctor. I didn't want to hurt people that knew and loved me anymore. But I would deal with that Monday because tonight was special. It was my 28th birthday and I knew Shunta had something special planned for me. I was full as hell and I needed to go upstairs and fuck the shit out of her before she got dressed because she said she had to go run a few errands before we left tonight. Damn I was so tired.

Janea Carter

Oh my God, last night was crazy. Jo said she wanted to talk to me before we went to the party. But I wasn't ready for what she told me at all. Jo confessed that she had a gambling problem for a long time and she had lost almost all our life savings. She was normally able to get the money back into our account before I noticed it was missing, but the problem had gotten worse. She also admitted that she had been seeing Dr. Johnson as a patient to deal with her addiction to gambling. She said she knew she wouldn't be able to face me without an explanation for where the money was. So she had sex with a drug dealer that she met at the gambling house. He always teased her about what he would do if she gave him a chance. He offered her large amounts of money. She made a deal with him. After they went to the bank and deposited the money that she had lost, they would go to the hotel.

She said he really enjoyed the fact that she was a lesbian. I knew that was something that Jo hated. Hell, it took me a while to penetrate her with the strap-on and it hurt her. I knew he hurt her. She said he got off on her pussy being so tight. He asked her is she had ever been with a man before and she told him the truth. She was a virgin when it came to men. Jo said that bastard had her in every position imaginable and that he didn't care that she was crying. She said she just kept looking at the clock, hoping it wouldn't be long before he finished his business. Her ordeal wasn't over until an hour later. She also said that he wouldn't use a condom and that he asked her for oral sex also, but she refused so he fucked her in her ass. That explained why she came home and took a shower immediately.

I was so shocked, I couldn't really reply. I was mad that she had to have sex with a man and I was also mad that she took our money without asking me. I explained that we would work it out and that I loved her. I really enjoyed being with her. I could tell Jo was hurt. She said she was making an appointment at Dr. White's office when I called her and she didn't click over because she didn't want to lose the receptionist on the other line. She said Dr. White was booked until next week, but she was on the waiting list, but they would call me if anyone canceled within the week.

After talking to Jo, I got dressed for Dr. White's surprise party. I bought the best suit, shoes and cologne money could buy. The suit and shoes were from the Purple Label Collection by Ralph

Lauren. The cologne was Polo Black by Ralph Lauren. Jo was so fine, I didn't even want to go to the party. I ordered my dress from Monif C. I saw her clothes once on Rip the Runway on BET. She catered to plus size women and I loved her clothes. Of course my purse and shoes came from the Jimmy Choo store in Peachtree Mall in Columbus. When we got to the Club, it was so packed that the valet had to park the car down the street. I wasn't sure who catered the party, but I wouldn't want it to be me. There were just too many people there. From the way the party looked outside, I knew we would have a good time once we got inside.

Shunta Thomas-White

Although I was mad as hell at Toni, I still loved her dearly. I still held on to the belief, however, that no matter how well you treated a person, they weren't promised to you. At any minute in life, you couldn't blink your eyes and things would be forever changed. I wasn't expecting it to change like this. The party was a huge success to some and to some, it wasn't. I finally got a chance to talk to Toni's sideline hoe, Trina. She said that Toni had promised her the world and she didn't deliver and she wasn't going to take it anymore. She had planned to confront Toni in front of me after the party. I just didn't want it to happen until after I thanked everybody for coming out. The mic would be open to anyone after that.

My mother finally arrived. Mrs. Thomas wanted to show everybody the side of Toni she knew. First she said a few nice things about Toni as far as how good she treated me in the beginning and that she was so grateful that Toni had everything set for me just in case something happened to her or Toni, I wouldn't have to worry about a thing. She showed pictures of me and Toni from the beginning of our relationship until the day we were married. Unfortunately, there weren't any pictures of the two us together after that.

My mother must have shown the whole crowd our whole life in pictures. Just when I thought I was finished looking at pictures, my mother picked up the microphone.

"Now that you have seen the good side of my daughter in law, Dr. Toni White, I would like you to see the not so good side of her."

Oh my God! The whole club stopped and just stood there with their mouths open in shock. There were so many pictures of Toni with other women. Most of them were patients in the room with their spouses. Toni and different women were on the pictures in every position there could be. But the real killer was when the video started. I simply looked over at Toni in disgust.

Toni had walked in the room where a patient was waiting to be seen. Toni came out with a cup of water and gave it to the patient. She then asked the patient a few questions and insisted that she drank the water. Toni and the patient, called Mrs. Carter, were talking about the pap exams and how important it was to get a regular pap exam. She was talking to Toni about her sisters and her getting their pap exams frequently because cervical cancer ran in their family and then the patient just stop talking. Toni then walked up between the patient's legs and put her hand in the patient's vaginal area. The patient didn't even move.

Mrs. Carter was at the party, too, and saw the video. She jumped up out of her seat.

"Oh my, God! That's me," she yelled angrily. She was so pretty. She even had the same Jimmy Choo bag as mine, but with a different color. I was stuck in my seat and couldn't move. The video shocked me. Mrs. Carter walked over to the table where Toni was seated.

Toni was as surprised as anyone was at the party. Her face was pale and she sweated heavily. She kept drinking and drinking, hoping that all of this was just a dream. She tried to apologize. Mrs. Carter picked up the glass of wine on the table in front of Toni and threw it in her face. She ran out of the club screaming she would sue the shit out of Toni. Jo looked at Toni who just sat there crying.

"You sick mother fucker!" Jo shouted. "I'll be back in here to kick your ass." Jo left and followed behind Mrs. Carter.

To my surprise no one in the room moved. They were watching the video like they were watching headline news. Toni started to eat Mrs. Carter's pussy right there on the table while she was in her office. Mrs. Carter had no clue what was happening to her, but Toni was having a field day. Toni was eating her and coming up and talking to her like she was actually talking back. Just when I thought it was over, Toni fucked her with her strap-on. I looked over at my mother and she was looking at Toni.

"Yeah, nigga! I got you now. You will never hurt my daughter again."

I never asked my mother where the videos or the pictures came from or how she even knew what was going on in Toni's office. I was hurt and didn't understand what was up with Toni. At the same time, I was happy. It had to end at some point. Toni was fucking everybody she could get her hands on. Everyone, except me. I was always the last one to know, but now I had the last laugh and so did other women, too.

STUD

She's a stud, but not so stud that I can't suck her
tits.
She's a stud, but not so stud that I can't lick her
clit.
She's a stud, but not too stud 'cause she cried out
in ecstasy from the orgasm she got from me.
She's a stud, but not too stud 'cause she watches
Lifetime movies with me.
She's a stud, but not so stud that I can't touch her
pussy softly.
She's a stud, but not so stud that she would
disrespect me.

Special Thanks

First, I would like to thank the Lord because I know all things are possible through Thee.

I want to give lots of love and thanks to my mother Amye Varnum. I know you didn't have a clue that I was writing a book. It wasn't because I was hiding anything from you, it's just at the time, I really just wanted to do something for me and other women that live the same life I live --"Lesbian." I know you don't agree with my lifestyle. However, I never noticed one change in the love you have for me and I thank you for that. If there is one thing you taught me, it was when you put your mind to something, stand by what you are doing and never be ashamed of what you are. You are truly my "shero."

Next, I would like to thank my family and friends for their support. Wow, who do I name first? It will have to be Lavonna "Strapp/TK" Collymore. Without you, I wouldn't have known I had the potential to write. Thanks for being there for me in the BEGINNING. It's funny how time changes people. I wish you all the best in the future and I pray you are happy in all of your endeavors.

I want to give thanks to my sister, my best friend, my homie, my shoulder to cry on, Ms. Leila Mcclenningham. Yes, L to the motherfucking A, LA. Girl, you read my stories over and over again and didn't have a clue about the lesbian lifestyle. When all my friends left, you stood by my side. You never once told me anything negative about my lifestyle. You looked at me as your friend and you stood by my side. It's so hard to come out to family and friends, but you listened to me over and over again and never once changed. I know you had some people questioning you for being by my side, but not once did you back away from me.

We have been through so much as friends, even trying to go back to school at our old age. I'm forever grateful that you are in my life. Many will try, but nothing will change our friendship. True friendship is so hard to come by. Everyone should look at you and I and enroll in a class taught by us. Let's call it "True Friendship 101." I Love you girl.

To my sister, Parthenia "Lefty" McGowan Jones, thanks for reading my stories and telling me how you felt about them. I really wanted to know your opinion and I know you can write, too. You should write a book next. Thanks again I love you. Thank you, Tecola "Cocoa" McGowan for reading my stories and just shaking your head. I guess that meant you liked them. Thanks for being patient with me and it's an honor to be one of your bridesmaids. I love you Black.

Wanda Forte, I just can't explain what you are to me. We have had some good times. We've laughed together and cried together. Thanks for always listening to me and telling me to pray and keep God first. You said I would find someone for me and not to give up. (She found me and I love her.) Kiss Quan for me and take care of my niece and my other nephews.

Thank you LaKasha (Keisha) Jackson. I wouldn't be in school today if it wasn't for you calling to see if I went or if I was on my way. I love you for that. When I was down, you told me not to give up. Thank you so much for giving me that song ME by Tamia. I must have played it until it wouldn't play anymore. It helped me so much. It's hard to find people that you can laugh and cry with in this day and time. Thanks for always believing in me and telling me I can do it. You didn't even know me that well and you opened your heart to be my friend at a time when I had stopped believing in the word "friend." Love you and take care of DJ.

Thank you Michelle (Twon) Slaughter for coming into my life. Girl, first of all thanks for those good phone conversations. I'm so happy I met you and I will always be here for you. Take care of my nieces and clear the calendar because we are about to party.

Thank you Wanda Hardie for making me feel like you had known me for years on my first day at work. When a person starts a new job, it's so important for them to feel comfortable and you made me feel that way. You were also one of the first people I told that I wanted to write a book. Thanks for reading my stories.

Thank you Gwen Whittaker for always being my co-worker/editor in the beginning and thanks for giving me advice when I didn't have a clue. Kiss Jennifer for me and tell her I can't wait to see her name all over the world because she will be famous.

To my other mother, Ms. Kewesi Alexandria St. James, I'm so blessed to have you in my life. You really treated me like a daughter. I love you so much. When I couldn't talk to anyone else, you were there for me. Thanks for allowing me to be your daughter and I hope you will always be my mother. The sky is the limit with the two most beautiful plus size women in the world. Smooches.

I would like to thank my family, the Berrengers. I love you all and thanks for accepting me into yours. To my father Mr. Altravious Berrenger Bonet, thanks for allowing me to be a part of your family. Special thanks to my brother, DaCrook Berrenger. I really needed to write another book just to tell you everything I wanted to tell you. I love you so much. Thanks for being my brother. Keep doing what you do because I love it, no matter what anyone else thinks?

To Mr. Hypnotic LaTweet, thanks for just being you. You have taught me a lot when it comes to loyalty and friendship. Some people just don't have your best interest at heart, no matter how much they smile at you. I want you to know that I am really a friend/sister to you and I always will whether you're partying all over Georgia or Alabama without me. I know, I know (Mess). I'm happy I got to work with you. Mrs. Tan Coleman, my friend, business partner, and sister, your spirit alone just brings me to tears. I'm so happy I was introduced to you. Who would have thought our partnership/friendship would grow this much? The sky is really the limit. We have prayed, partied, cried, and laughed together and you are still the same person. Thanks for believing in me. When I couldn't see my own potential, you saw it and pushed me even further. Thanks for being there. I know you will be at the top with me. THE RAINBOW CONNECTION is where we started this friendship and I know it will continue to grow. Kisses to you from my Lips to your Tulips (You know what that means. HA, HA, HA).

Pamela "Coogi" Fulton, there aren't enough words to express how much I love and appreciate you. Sometimes we think that we are alone in this world of destruction and then there comes an angel to help with things that we thought just couldn't be fixed. Thanks for always believing in me. When I couldn't see a way out, you showed me. When I was about to do things to get myself on the "blotter," as you called it, you talked to me and told me that's not the path to go on. You believed in me, all of me, and not in the hype of the name FINA. I love you and if I said anything else, it would be a "misunderstanding" to some people. Thanks for allowing me to be a part of MarKayla "Luda" Marshall's life. I love her so much. I will always be here for her. Thanks for helping me make difficult choices. I know you didn't have to, but you did it because you have just that much love for me. WOW!! I'm still amazed by you and all you do.

Always honor me with your presence because I truly love everything about you, even when you are mean as hell in the morning.

I would like to thank all the women in my life who have inspired me to write a book about our lifestyle as seen through my eyes. Thanks to the following for your contribution to my dream of writing a book: Another Family Affair, Natalia King, Noetic Inveigling, Ltd, Sheena Jones, Maria Williams and Damion Brumfield a.k.a Dijone and Maria Brumfield. Damion, your advice has helped me greatly, not just from a business standpoint. You have helped me with my relationships and you have always been sincere with your advice. For that, I'm truly thankful.

I would like to thank my daughter, Eboni Milsap. I will never forget how you helped me with your brothers when it was only the four of us. I love you and I wish you all the best in life. Whenever you call me, I'm coming. Remember *the Color Purple:* "Nothing but death could keep me from it." I always have your best interest in mind. Although you feel I don't allow you to do much, remember that ma loves you. I know we are just alike in so many ways. We keep our true feelings in so that our heart is protected. No matter how we try to act with each other, we know we are each other's biggest fans. I love you so, so, much.

Thank you O'Shay "Man" Jones for never being too old to show your mother love. I love your hugs and kisses. I can't wait to see you in the NBA. I'm going to be on the front row screaming "that's my boy." I love you so much. You are a good boy and I know you are going to make an excellent husband and father. But not yet. I pray that you stay just like you are now-silly as hell.

Andre' "Duke" Collins Jr., you are supposed to be my baby. You have grown up so much that you don't even need me anymore, which bring me to tears. I love you dearly. You have really grown up. Always keep your head to the sky and thanks for always wanting to be bothered with your nagging mother. When I wanted to watch *The Color Purple* over and over again, you would watch it with me like it was your first time all the time. I love you for that.

Kimberly "Na-Na" Thornton, YOU ARE OFFICALLY my daughter. I can't believe it. I hope I'm everything a mother can be to a daughter for you. I love you and thanks for allowing me to be your mother. I'm so proud of you for going back to school and working. I knew you could do it. Just when I thought I wasn't going to have a daughter that needed me anymore since Eboni turned 18, the Lord blessed me with you. I love all the hugs and thanks for opening up to me. I know, I know. Yeah, yeah, yeah!!

La Sonia "LA" Walton, thanks for reading my work. I know you were tired of me asking you to read it, but you still did it. I'm glad you finally started to talk. Remember to keep your head up. Thanks for allowing me to be your mother.

Yasmin "Boozse" Perry, thanks for accepting me as your mother. I love you. Stay focused on school and stay out of trouble. I can't wait to see you walk the aisle with your diploma.

Javairia "Nu-Nu" Smith, in the beginning, you called me "Ma." You are so beautiful, even when you are mad at me. I wish you all the best in life and if you ever really need me, I will be there. But, you have to make the first move.

Takethia "Shayboo" Moore, thanks for being in my family. I know you are going to go far in life. I can't wait to see you in the WNBA. Stay focused.

Temecka "Slim" Simpson, words can't express the love I have for you. You were my first child and boy you were a handful. I love you and you will always have a place in my heart. NOTHING WILL EVER CHANGE THAT.

Derricka "Pitt" Lewis, thanks for coming into my life. You will be in my heart forever. Make sure you take care of Cameron. I love you both.

To my publisher, Sharon of Seven Stages Publishing, thanks for being so patient with me. I remember our first conversation. You promised you would help me and you did. Sometimes all a person needs is a chance and you gave me mine. Thank you.